"Now, let's get down to business, shall we. I've heard good things about you. Good things. I have a special assignment for you. You can prove your worth. Big reward possible. Big reward."

Hiding the fact that Mr. Sampson's repetitive speech was beginning to get on her nerves, Colleen smiled and looked at him expectantly. He looked at her expectantly. The silence in the room seemed interminable until she realized that he was waiting for a response from her.

"Yes, Mr. Sampson?"

"A woman who respects authority. I like that. Now, we have a claim that came in a couple of weeks ago. A big claim. One and a half million smackers to be exact. Big, wouldn't you say?"

"Yes, very big," she answered obediently.

"Some bodybuilder type went and got herself killed in Rehoboth Beach. Police say it was an accident — as in case closed — but Fidelity Life and Casualty suspects murder or suicide."

A female bodybuilder? In Rehoboth Beach? This could prove interesting, Colleen thought. "Who are the beneficiaries?"

He rifled through some papers in a manila folder. "Yes, here it is," he exclaimed, pulling a sheet of paper from the stack. "There are only two, the deceased's business partner, a guy by the name of Stephan Gray. Oh yes, and a friend named Lori Kestler." He drew out the word *friend* like it was the punchline of a dirty joke. "Makes you suspicious right there, eh?"

"Sir?"

"Oh come on, Colleen. A same-sex friend beneficiary? Something queer going on there, if you know what I mean. Something queer." He winked conspiratorially.

About the Author

Barbara Johnson turns 40 this year, and thanks the goddess that for 22 of those years she has shared her life with Kathleen. They share their Maryland home with three cats and three birds. Barbara is busy working on two more novels to be published by Naiad, *Valentine Moon* and *Ravenswood*, the long-awaited sequel to *Stonehurst*.

THE
Beach Affair

A Novel by

Barbara Johnson

THE NAIAD PRESS, INC.
1995

Printed in the United States of America on acid-free paper
First Edition

Editor: Christine Cassidy
Cover designer: Bonnie Liss (Phoenix Graphics)
Typesetter: Sandi Stancil

Library of Congress Cataloging-in-Publication Data

Johnson, Barbara, 1955 –
   The beach affair / Barbara Johnson.
      p.   cm.
   ISBN 1-56280-090-6 (pbk.)
   I. Title.
PS3560.037174B43   1995
813'.54—dc20   95-16180
                                                    CIP

For Kathleen
My One True Love

Acknowledgments

I would like to thank my lover, Kathleen DeBold, whose invaluable advice and support guided me once more through the creative process. Thanks to Christine Cassidy, my editor, as always, a great help. I've received wonderful support from all my friends, but I'd like particularly to thank those who encouraged (i.e., nagged) me more than most: Becky, Cindy, Deborah, Dori Anne, Jim, Julie, Karl, and Peggy. An additional thanks to Julie and Joan, who provided additional Rehoboth Beach particulars.

Thanks also to the following people, who lent their personalities: Amy, Babo, Deanna, Jessica, Pat, and Peg.

I was fortunate to do booksignings for my first book, *Stonehurst,* at the following bookstores: 31st Street Bookstore (Baltimore, MD), Lammas (D.C.), OutRight Books (Virginia Beach, VA), Phoenix Rising (Richmond, VA), Out & About Books (Orlando, FL), and HerStory Bookstore (Hallam, PA). I thank them all for giving an unknown writer with a debut novel the opportunity to meet new people and gain new experiences.

And finally, I would also like to thank the following gay-friendly or gay-owned businesses in Rehoboth Beach who have graciously given permission to use their real names: Blue Moon, Dream Café, Lambda Rising, Mano's, Paper Nautilus, Sand in My Shoes, Splash, and Square One. The Paper Nautilus, however, is no longer a B&B, but is now a wonderful Mexican restaurant called Dos Locos. If you have an occasion to visit Rehoboth, please patronize these businesses and tell them you read about them in *The Beach Affair.*

Prologue

Candy Emerson breathed the tangy, salty sea air as she walked along the wooden boardwalk to her gym. It was barely light, still too early for most anyone else to be up and about. She paused to watch some gulls attacking a crab scuttling about the sand, one of the unlucky few exposed with the retreat of the tide. The birds fought briefly over the tasty morsel before one screeched triumphantly and sailed away over the dark water. Candy grimaced slightly before continuing her walk. The gym shoes she wore squeaked, but muffled her footsteps on the old wood.

At this far end of the boardwalk, no bright patches of new wood marred its weather-beaten surface. The last hurricane had seen fit to damage the south end where the gay men gathered. Some of the townspeople chose to see it as an omen, and they hoped it would keep the gays away. Candy laughed out loud. It would take more than a broken boardwalk to keep the pretty boys from working on their tans.

The hair on her neck prickled as she heard running footsteps behind her. Since the gay bashing that had occurred a couple of weeks ago, everyone was on edge. She turned her head as the footsteps came closer, then smiled nervously and let out a deep breath when she saw the runner. It was Mr. Anderson who lived on Rodney Street. Seventy years old, and he still jogged every morning no matter what the weather. He waved enthusiastically as he swept past.

Almost to the end of the boardwalk, Candy stopped in front of Bodies By the Beach, the gym she owned. She breathed a sigh of relief to see that its plate glass window had survived yet another night. Anti-gay sentiment was rising in the town, and at least three other gay-owned businesses had been recently vandalized. She'd thought about getting those metal, barred storefront protectors, but that seemed such a drastic measure, and an expensive one. Still, she was cautious as she put the key in the lock. She opened the door and turned on the lights, alert for any movement. Of course there was none. She was getting paranoid. She entered the gym and locked the door carefully behind her.

Candy immediately turned off the alarm and then the harsh overhead lights; for her solitary workout, she preferred the more subdued night lights. She was surprised to see used towels and free weights scattered around the carpet in the workout area — she'd have to talk to Stephan about making sure that everything was in order when he closed up at night. He'd been getting a little careless lately. She concluded he must have been totally distracted last night, and hoped he hadn't gotten bad news about Phillip.

In a hurry to get started, Candy decided to leave the mess alone and went directly to the women's locker room. She stripped off her burgundy and gold sweats — Washington Redskins colors — and tucked the bottom of her white muscle T into her purple and black gym shorts. She put a terrycloth headband around her forehead, buckled her weight belt loosely around her waist, and put on a new pair of weight-training gloves. She rummaged through her gym bag for her bottle of Evian, then grabbed a fresh towel off the rack and headed to the workout area.

In the dim light, the room was almost gloomy; the Nautilus equipment stood like silent sentinels in the eerie quiet. Candy couldn't shake a feeling of unease, but she controlled her jitters and got down to business. Just because she'd retired from professional bodybuilding didn't mean she would let her hard, muscled body go soft. She did a few light exercises — stretches, calisthenics, some light weight work, the stationary bike — making sure she could feel the warmth penetrating her muscles. When she felt ready to lift, she loaded two twenty-five-pound plates onto a forty-five-pound barbell and settled it into the grooved holders above the flat bench. She tightened her weight belt carefully and then lay on her back with her legs on either side of the bench. She knew that Stephan would be annoyed that she hadn't waited for him, but she'd been restless that morning and couldn't sleep. Stephan had to know that she'd never do any really heavy lifting without a spotter, but she expected he'd give her the mandatory lecture on the dangers of working out alone when he arrived.

Candy lifted the barbell above her head and, inhaling loudly but evenly, brought the bar to her chest. A full exhale and the weight went up. She repeated the lift fourteen more times and then returned the weight to rest in the grooves. She rested only a few minutes before starting a set with twenty pounds more weight. She followed with a third set, then a fourth, adding ten more pounds each time. She sat up and shook out her arms. Only three more sets to go. Candy loved the way her body responded to pyramiding — increasing the weight a little each time and cranking out the reps. She could feel the blood pulsing through her veins, her muscles expanding as they pumped up. The rush it gave her was a physical high that no drug could replicate. She felt incredibly strong and powerful. Her body tingled, and she had the sensation of floating. She added ten more pounds to the bar and lay back down. She closed her eyes and concentrated on her breathing, wanting to block out all distractions.

She raised the barbell and suddenly felt a sharp pain on her arm. Her muscle spasmed and the weight hit her chest, knocking the breath out of her. Her eyes flew open, but her vision was only a blur. Panicked, she struggled to get a grip on the barbell, but it eluded her. It rolled from her chest to her neck, crushing her windpipe. The pressure increased.

She tried to gasp for air, but none came. She clawed at the barbell, her torso and legs moving violently as she tried to extricate herself from the heavy iron stranglehold. Another electric pain shot through her arm. Her body went limp, her arms hanging at her sides. Paralyzed, she felt the weight press down. Harder. A bright red light exploded behind her eyes, then blackness.

CHAPTER 1

Lisa Anderson stuck her head into Colleen Fitzgerald's cramped office. "The boss wants to see you," she said. At Colleen's unspoken question, Lisa shrugged her shoulders and raised her eyebrows before she left the room.

Sighing, Colleen pulled her rumpled linen jacket over her white cotton blouse and rose from her chair. The fan on the floor in front of her desk made her Indian cotton skirt billow into a bell around her legs. She pulled her hair out of its ponytail as she trudged up the long hallway, passing several offices that were just like her own — cramped and dingy and devoid of natural light. The faded brown carpet was stained, the walls a dirty white. The harsh fluorescent lighting did little to hide the dreariness of the downtown office building that was like so many others. And the air conditioning was on the fritz again. Colleen could feel the sweat begin to trickle between her breasts. God, another sweltering July day in our nation's capital. If she didn't get out of town soon, she would surely perish from the heat and humidity.

She passed through a pair of glass doors and immediately the decor changed. The walls shone with new mauve paint; the plush mauve carpeting matched exactly. Fine reproductions of famous works of art hung in perfect symmetry on the walls, and potted plants held strategic positions. The Muzak wasn't as loud here as in Colleen's area of the building. She rounded the corner and came to a halt in a large airy room. Two secretaries sat at separate desks on either side. One was on the phone. Colleen could hear his voice, soothing and low, as if he were comforting a small child. The other secretary stood on tiptoe and watered a trailing philodendron that perched on top of a file cabinet. Her tight black miniskirt crept up her thighs. Nice legs, Colleen thought fleetingly as she approached the man talking on the phone.

Obviously annoyed at the interruption, he looked up and covered the phone with his hand. "May I help you?"

"I'm Colleen Fitzgerald." The secretary looked at her blankly. "Mr. Sampson wants to see me."

"Just go in. He's on the phone, but shouldn't be

long. Talking to his wife." He waved his hand in dismissal and turned his attention back to the call.

"Thanks," Colleen said, rolling her eyes as she turned her back. Some people are just so professional, she thought.

She hesitated a few moments before knocking on the closed door that had "MR. KEVIN SAMPSON" emblazoned on it in gold. In the six months that she'd worked at Sampson and Rhoades Investigations, she'd only seen Mr. Sampson once — at her orientation. He gave some cliché-ridden speech about what a wonderful place Sampson and Rhoades was and if everyone kept "his nose to the grindstone" and was a team player they would all enjoy the fruits of their labors. She couldn't imagine why he would want to see her — a novice investigator, fresh out of school with a degree in Police Science. She hoped she hadn't screwed something up already. At Mr. Sampson's "Come in," Colleen self-consciously ran her fingers through her wavy hair, willing it to lie somewhat flat. She had to get to a salon, and soon.

The spacious office, with one wall made entirely of glass, afforded a panoramic view of the Potomac River. She saw dozens of boats on the river and wished she was in one of them. She glanced around the room, taking in the expensive new wallpaper, the enormous oak desk, the elaborate computer setup, and the credenza that she would bet hid a full bar.

The man behind the desk was also huge and reminded her of silent movie star Fatty Arbuckle. He wore an expensive but ill-fitting smoke-gray suit. His white shirt was rumpled and stained with what appeared to be tomato sauce. His tie was the most hideous thing Colleen had ever seen — wide and pea green with what seemed to be black and white naked women cavorting across it. She was instantly offended, and averted her eyes to stare at the ostentatious gold pen and pencil set that sat precariously on the front edge of the desk. Seized by an uncontrollable urge to knock it off, she angled her body so she could "accidentally" bump it. Before she could accomplish her mission, Mr. Sampson slammed down the telephone receiver and startled her.

"Sit down! Sit down, Miss Fitzgerald!" his booming voice crashed into her ears. "Or may I call you Colleen? Nice Irish name, that. Nice Irish name."

"Colleen will be fine, Mr. Sampson." She sat gingerly on the edge of a black leather chair that faced his desk.

"Good. Good. Now, let's get down to business, shall we. I've heard good things about you. Good things. I have a special assignment for you. You can prove your worth. Big reward possible. Big reward."

Hiding the fact that Sampson's repetitive speech was beginning to get on her nerves, she smiled and looked at him expectantly. He looked at her expectantly. The silence in the room seemed interminable until she realized that he was waiting for a response from her.

"Yes, Mr. Sampson?"

"A woman who respects authority. I like that. Now, we have a claim that came in a couple of weeks ago. A big claim. One and a half million smackers to be exact. Big, wouldn't you say?"

"Yes, very big," she answered obediently.

"Some bodybuilder type went and got herself killed in Rehoboth Beach. Police say it was an accident — as in case closed — but Fidelity Life and Casualty suspects murder or suicide."

A female bodybuilder? In Rehoboth Beach? This could prove interesting, Colleen thought. She asked, "Why don't they believe the police? Surely they investigated?"

"All this money involved? And an accidental death rider that doubles the amount to three mil? They don't *want* to believe the police."

Colleen nodded in understanding. "Who are the beneficiaries?"

He rifled through some papers in a manila folder. "Yes, here it is," he exclaimed, pulling a sheet of paper from the stack. "There are only two, the deceased's business partner, a guy by the name of Stephan Gray. Oh yes, and a friend named Lori Kestler." He drew out the word *friend* like it was the punchline of a dirty joke. "Makes you suspicious right there, eh?"

"Sir?"

"Oh come on, Colleen. A same-sex friend beneficiary? Something queer going on there, if you know what I mean. Something queer." He winked conspiratorially.

She ground her teeth and clenched her cotton skirt into an ironing nightmare. This man was making her sick, but he was her boss and she knew she didn't have the courage to take him to task. She controlled her anger. "What do you want me to do?"

He shoved the folder at her. "Read this. I'm sending you to Rehoboth Beach to ask some questions and get the answers Fidelity wants. I want you there ASAP so we can get this one settled and out of here."

"Shouldn't this go to a more experienced investigator?"

"You've been here long enough and I've heard good things about you. Time to prove just how tough you are. Just how tough. Besides, everyone else is on vacation or already on a case. I'll send someone else if you don't have this wrapped up within a week or so. Any more questions?"

Before she had a chance to answer, he picked up the phone and dialed a number. It was his dismissal. With a bad taste in her mouth, Colleen grabbed the folder and hurried out of the room. The two secretaries in the outer office were in the exact same positions as when she'd first come in. Only now the one on the phone was speaking more heatedly and the plant waterer was snipping off dead leaves. Nice jobs, Colleen thought as she headed out the glass doors and back into the dreary world of peons.

When Colleen got back to her office, Lisa was waiting for her, perched on the edge of Colleen's desk, and showing off lots of leg in the red miniskirt she was barely wearing. Don't any of the women around here believe in pants, Colleen thought grumpily as she put the folder into her briefcase. She'd been single for more than a year and celibacy was beginning to wear on her. Determined not to waste her time ogling her straight co-worker, she poured herself a mug of coffee from the small coffee maker on her file cabinet, then watched as a Klingon Bird of Prey materialized on her Star Trek mug.

"So, are you fired or what?" Lisa asked with characteristic bluntness.

"Is that the only thing that happens when people go into Mr. Sampson's office?"

"No," Lisa wisecracked. "Now that you mention it, some people he puts on probation."

Colleen laughed. "Well, I am not fired or on probation. I'm on special assignment."

Lisa leaped off the desk. "Special assignment? How'd you rate that?"

"He said he had good reports about me and it's my chance to prove my mettle. So, I'm going to Rehoboth to check out a suspicious claim."

"Rehoboth? Man, I don't believe this. You get to go to the beach? In July?" Lisa started to pace the room, her long tapered fingers glued to her shapely hips. She was so annoyed that she spit as she talked. "I've been here longer than you!" She started making clucking noises as she paced. Colleen expected her arms to start flapping at any minute.

"I know exactly why Mr. Sampson picked me over you," Colleen said soothingly. "This is an open-and-shut case. You have a lot more experience than I do, so he wants you here to take care of more important things."

Colleen's attempt to calm her friend didn't work. "Great! This is just great. I'm being punished for being a good worker!!" Lisa kept clucking as she walked back and forth in front of Colleen's desk, but she didn't flap her arms.

"Look, I'm sorry, Lisa," Colleen said finally, "but

I need to get back to work. I have a few things to finish up before I go. Do you mind?"

"Just wait until Janis hears about this."

Oh great, Colleen thought. Janis was only the biggest gossip in the office. Well, she couldn't worry about that now. " 'Bye, Lisa. Have a good week."

The leggy brunette stalked out of Colleen's office, but forgot to slam the door. Colleen sighed, and then let a grin spread across her face. What luck! Rehoboth in the summertime! One of the gay meccas of the Atlantic coast. She decided to stop at Lambda Rising Bookstore on the way home to pick up a lesbian travel guide. Maybe she could find a good gay-owned bed-and-breakfast. This could turn out to be the best thing that ever happened to her.

She glanced at the clock. Still one hour before quitting time. She got her briefcase and fished out the manila folder. Might as well read up on what she was supposed to do. She sat at her desk and sipped the scalding hot coffee.

The file was kind of skimpy. It contained the original insurance policy, a copy of Candy Emerson's will, the death certificate, a summary of the police report, letters from both beneficiaries, and a couple of newspaper clippings.

Bodies By the Beach owner, Candy Emerson, was found dead early one morning at the gym by her business partner. Official cause of death: a 245-pound barbell had fallen on her, crushing her chest and strangling her. Colleen grimaced as she read the gruesome details. Didn't these weightlifter types usually have partners to prevent stuff like that from happening? She tried to visualize something that weighed 245 pounds. Would it be like lifting a couch?

13

A washing machine? It was impossible for Colleen to imagine lifting that much weight — her own over-fed cat seemed heavy at just fifteen pounds.

The police report certainly supported the accidental death claim. The victim was apparently capable of lifting 245 pounds and was known to work out alone. When her partner, Stephan Gray, arrived at the gym at six-thirty, he saw the words "Dyke Bitch" scrawled across the window, but no other signs of trespass or forced entry. Hmmm, she thought, was that where Mr. Sampson's "something queer" remark had come from?

After Gray turned on the lights and walked into the workout area, he saw the victim and ran to her aid. But she was clearly dead. Gray claimed he touched nothing and called the police immediately. No evidence of burglary. The cash register was untouched, nothing was missing, and the police found the victim's set of keys to the gym in her gym bag.

The victim's smeared fingerprints and blood from her torn fingernails were all over the barbell, bench, and plates. Results of latent fingerprinting and scene analysis were inconclusive — which was to be expected given the number of people who used the gym each day.

Colleen's mind flashed back to the slides of strangulation victims that were shown in one of her classes. She shook the grisly images out of her head and finished reading the report before she called the actuarial tables up on her computer. Death by barbell. She scanned the files.

Suspicious strangulations in prisons. Convicted murderers dropping weights on each other. An irate woman smashed a twenty-pound dumbbell into her husband's groin while he was bench pressing, which caused him to drop the weight and crush his windpipe. Lots of people beating each other's heads in with barbells and dumbbells. Fights over equipment.

None of these bloody scenarios fit this case. According to the police report, Candy's body had no marks other than those caused by the barbell and by her thrashing around to free herself. Colleen wished she had the actual autopsy report. It was possible the police had missed something that the coroner would have found.

After thoroughly checking the files on murder, attempted murder, and vicious assault, Colleen considered the possibility of suicide. Suicide within two years of a new policy automatically voided it, and Candy's policy was only twenty-three months old. But the particulars of this case, combined with the fact that there were no documented cases of suicide by barbell, made suicide seem like wishful thinking by Fidelity. Three million dollars was a lot of money for the company to have to shell out, and Colleen had seen insurance companies stonewall payment on valid claims for as little as a hundred grand.

She moved onto the beneficiaries. Candy's business partner, Stephan Gray. What could be his motives? Unrequited love for Candy? A business deal gone sour? Gambling addiction? Drugs? Just a plain old quarrel that got out of hand? And the other one, Lori Kestler. Friend. Colleen had to agree with her boss that "friend" often equaled "lover" on these policies. Lots of possibilities there. Jealousy. A jilted lover. An affair discovered. A rival. Perhaps the relationship broke up and Lori wanted the money before Candy changed the policy? Colleen had already seen that situation several times before. And the graffiti on the window would certainly seem to indicate that Candy *was* gay, or at least someone thought so. She decided to hold off on further speculation until she'd had a chance to interview Gray and Kestler and check their backgrounds.

Colleen poured a second cup of coffee before she unfolded the newspaper clippings. "Female Body-builder Found Dead" and "Musclewoman Meets Tragic Fate." The accounts contained no new information about Candy's death, but did provide some insight about her life.

It seemed that Candy Emerson's bodybuilding career began as a young girl with an interest in gymnastics. In her early teens, told she was too tall and bulky to compete in her chosen sport, she turned to weight training and wanted to try wrestling. That too was denied her because girls were not allowed to compete in a "male" sport. Undaunted, Candy continued working with weights and discovered a talent for track and field, where her strength gave her an advantage with the discus and javelin. In college, she majored in physical education and was encouraged by her coach to try powerlifting. She won a few local competitions, but within five years had turned to bodybuilding. Her meteoric rise to champion was apparently legendary.

She won several world championships before winning the coveted Ms. Olympic Universe an unprecedented three times in a row. She then retired from professional bodybuilding to open Bodies By The Beach, a health club on the boardwalk in Rehoboth Beach. She was 41 years old when she died.

No surviving relatives listed. Nothing about a

husband or boyfriend. Colleen thought about her own family — all four grandparents still alive, both parents, two siblings with children, various aunts and uncles and cousins. Odd that Candy had no other relatives. The articles made no mention of family history.

The newspaper photos were not very clear, but the woman looked to be very attractive. Big, blonde, and most definitely tanned.

To Colleen, she looked to be extraordinarily tall. The classic bodybuilding pose showed off broad shoulders and a heavily muscled body. It was a little too much bulk for Colleen's taste. Candy's breasts in the skimpy bikini seemed nonexistent. That was definitely not to Colleen's liking. Still, Colleen didn't think she'd turn down an opportunity to date someone like Candy. She kind of liked the somewhat masculine look about her.

Colleen closed the Emerson file. Candy was obviously a celebrity in the world of bodybuilding, but Colleen had never heard of her and she knew nothing of the sport. It always seemed like too much work. To be honest, any exercise seemed like too much work to her. She knew that she should do something — walk or swim or take aerobics classes. At twenty-seven, she sort of took her body for granted, but did notice that her weight was creeping up. The days were gone when she could eat anything she wanted and not gain an ounce. She read all the magazine articles that said exercise was essential to healthy living. Heck, Sampson and Rhoades put out brochures about the same thing. She pictured the portly Mr. Sampson and smiled at the realization that she wasn't the only employee ignoring the company's advice. Well, at least she was a vegetarian — that should count for something. Thinking about her body reminded her that she'd need to buy a bathing suit for this trip. Maybe that would induce her to swim?

The jangling of the telephone startled Colleen out of a silent argument over whether to get a one-piece or a bikini. She knocked over her coffee mug as she reached for the phone. The Klingon Bird of Prey disappeared as the hot liquid spilled over her blotter. She grabbed a couple fistfuls of Kleenex to soak up the coffee.

"Colleen Fitzgerald," she managed to shout into the phone.

"I'm not hard of hearing yet," her mother admonished.

"Sorry, Mom," Colleen replied. "I just spilled coffee all over my desk. What's up?"

"Your father and I want to go away for a few days next week. Do you think you could come by the house a couple of times and check to be sure everything is okay?"

"Can't help you out this time." Colleen silently thanked her luck. Driving out of the city and around the beltway to Gaithersburg was not her idea of fun. "Sampson and Rhoades is sending me away on assignment. I have to go to Delaware for a couple of weeks."

"Delaware? What's in Delaware?"

"I'm investigating a case, Mom. That's my job, remember?"

"They don't usually send you away. Can't you postpone this? I don't want to have to ask your brother."

Colleen blotted the tissue more furiously. "He

18

lives a lot closer to you than I do. You two at least live in the same state."

Her mother let out an exasperated sigh. "He's got a family, you know. He can't be leaving all the time to come up here."

"Well, I can't this time either, Mother." She took a deep breath before adding, "And I really wish you wouldn't keep thinking that just because I'm single, I have no life of my own."

"Don't use that testy tone of voice with me, young lady. And don't forget to send a postcard."

The dial tone buzzed in Colleen's ear. She cradled the receiver gently. She loved her parents dearly, but they refused to lose their dependence on her. Her brother, William, lived only ten miles from them, but the fact that he had a wife and kids seemed to make him immune to their needs. So she ended up house-sitting and petsitting and babysitting and gardening and chauffeuring and delivering — doing all those support jobs that lesbians always seem to do for their families. How dare the right-wing homophobes say we have no family values, she thought angrily. It's the families that don't realize *our* value!

Colleen glanced at the clock. 4:55. She wasn't going to wait five lousy minutes, so she turned off her computer and straightened up her desk. Well, she mused, at least her family had stopped asking her when she would be getting married. Wouldn't they be surprised if they knew their nice Catholic girl was a lesbian? Or perhaps she didn't give them enough credit. Maybe they did know.

She stuffed the Emerson file back into her briefcase, turned off the coffee maker, and headed for the Metro.

CHAPTER 2

The Metro seemed more crowded than usual that Tuesday afternoon, more like a Friday. A short man in a rumpled business suit and sneakers knocked Colleen's briefcase out of her arms just as she went to sit down. She had to scurry after it before it got trampled. When she got back to the seat, the short man had taken it. She gave him her best "you're an asshole" glare. He ignored her.

As the train rumbled from one stop to the next, Colleen started planning for her trip. If she could, she would head out to Rehoboth on Thursday and beat the weekend traffic. So many details to attend to. Who would take care of her cat, for one thing. A kennel would be too expensive and it made her feel guilty to think of Smokey locked up in kitty prison. Maybe she could convince her friend Brian to stop by once a day on his way home. That way, she wouldn't have to put a hold on the *Washington Post* or make arrangements at the post office for her mail. The plants would be okay for a week, maybe two. It certainly would be nice to stretch the assignment out to at least two weeks.

The seemingly endless subway ride finally over, Colleen got out at DuPont Circle. It always made her happy to step off the subway escalator and find herself in the midst of gay D.C. What a stroke of luck she'd had to find a rent-controlled efficiency in one of the city's premier areas.

The air was humid, and Colleen broke out in a sweat. She could practically feel her hair start to curl. A homeless man wearing a tattered "No Newt is Good Newt" T-shirt approached her.

"How are you tonight, Jake?" she asked, handing him a dollar bill.

"Jus' fine," he answered as he took the money. "Thanks to you, as always. God bless you."

As he turned his attention to the man behind her, Colleen headed across the street. Although the Q Street exit was closer to her home, she always got off on the far side of Connecticut Avenue so she could walk across the circle. People of all kinds occupied the grassy areas or sat on the low wall of the fountain. The homeless sat next to yuppies who sat next to bicycle messengers on break. Gays and straights mingled in seeming harmony, while at permanent stone tables old white men played chess with young black students. Colleen liked to think of DuPont Circle as a place where people forgot their differences, a space shared by those who drank their white zinfandel out of crystal glasses and those who drank their Mad Dog out of bottles hidden in brown paper bags.

She walked slowly around the fountain. A black Labrador puppy wearing a rainbow bandanna was romping in the water. He was splashing everyone, but no one seemed to care. Smiling, she paused to watch the puppy's antics and then continued her stroll past the fountain, out of the circle, and onto Connecticut Avenue. She stopped to admire the colorful window display at Lambda Rising Bookstore before stepping inside.

"Hey Brian," she called to the man behind the counter. "How goes it?"

"Not too bad. Been kind of a slow day. Everyone must still be at the beach I guess."

"Speaking of the beach ... I'm being sent to Rehoboth on assignment. How's that for a coup?"

"Lucky girl."

"What do you think my chances are of getting a room at this late date?"

"About the same as me getting a date with Brad Pitt."

"I was afraid of that."

"This time of year even the straight hotels are full. Anything available can get expensive."

"Well, I'm not worried; my company's picking up the tab." Colleen chose a travel guide, then popped the question. "So, how would you like to catsit for Smokey while I'm gone?"

"I don't know. Do you think a little pussy will ruin my reputation?"

"Brian!"

"Of course I will. I'll stop by later tonight and you can fill me in on what to do."

"Thanks. He's really a good cat."

"If I were you, darling," Brian cut in, "I'd forget about the beast and concentrate on the babes. When was the last time you got laid?"

Colleen blushed, but before she could answer him a customer approached and took his attention. Colleen browsed the women's best-sellers, then selected a mystery and a romance.

"So, what's your assignment at the beach anyway?" Brian asked as he rang up her purchases.

"I'm investigating a suspicious death. A female bodybuilder. Really bizarre kind of case."

"Yeah, I heard about it. Candy Apple or something, right?"

"Candy Emerson."

"Yeah, well my friends at the beach tell me that she was a lesbian. You gonna try to find out who murdered her?"

"Murder? The police report calls it an accidental death."

Brian gave a snort of derision. "Do you really think the police care if one more queer is dead? If her throat was cut they'd find a way to say it was an accident."

She took the change he handed her. "Who do people at the beach think killed her?"

He shrugged. "I just hear things in passing. Maybe people are overreacting because of the gay bashings. The cops could care less."

"Yes, but murder is different. They have to take it seriously."

He shrugged again. He'd already lost several friends to AIDS and even one friend to gay bashers.

"Brian, are you going to the gym tonight?"

"Of course. Bodies like mine are made, not born."

"Can you do me a favor?"

"Bring you back a hot little butch? I thought you'd never ask. There is this cute personal trainer, she's —"

Colleen cut him off. Since her breakup with Amy, Brian had fixed her up with enough of his psycho-dyke friends to last a lifetime. "Can you just bring me some of those bodybuilding magazines if you see any?"

"Yes mistress," he said, feigning annoyance as he turned to the next customer. His eyes lit up with pleasure.

She glanced at the tall, well-muscled man standing at the counter. His complexion was the color of creamy hot chocolate, and short rasta locks framed perfectly molded features. She smiled as she heard the purr in Brian's voice. He made "Can I help you?" sound like an intimate invitation.

Colleen grabbed a copy of the *Washington Blade* and made her way home. The ivy-covered, red brick building was a source of great comfort to her. She had first arrived in Washington six months ago during the coldest February in history, yet even then the building had seemed to absorb the warmth of the sun and glow cheerfully through the snow. Six steps led to the entrance, and she used her key to open the glass-paneled door. In the marbled entry way, she got her mail, grimacing at the bills and junk mail.

Thinking of her new bathing suit, she decided to walk up the six flights rather than take the elevator. By the fourth floor, she regretted her decision. She really needed to do something to get into shape. Her condition was almost embarrassing.

As soon as she put her key in the lock, the cat started meowing. Colleen kicked the door open with her foot.

"Hello, Smokey," she crooned as she bent to pet the Russian Blue that wound around her legs. He stood on his hind legs and swatted at her hand. It was his way of looking for the dried anchovies she sometimes fed him as a treat.

"You are a bad kitty," she said, frowning when she spied an overturned plant on the window sill. "No fish for you today." She put her bag and briefcase on the coffee table and sat down on the black and white striped bed couch to listen to her phone messages.

Beep. "Hi, Colleen. This is your sister. Just want to remind you that your niece turns five this Saturday. If you haven't gotten her anything yet, she really wants the Wedding Barbie. Just in case you need ideas. Mom sent money again. Like Andrea really cares about money at her age. Call. Don't forget, we're three hours behind here in Portland. 'Bye. Oh, can you call William and remind him too. About Andrea, I mean. Thanks, I'll talk to you later."

Some things never change, Colleen thought. Meagan must think she was made of money. The Wedding Barbie indeed. Well, Andrea would have to be happy with the Osh Kosh overalls and the stuffed alligator she'd already sent.

Beep. "Hey, Col. Amy. Look, I know you said you

gave me everything, but I'm missing every single k.d. lang CD. You know I never lose anything, so you must still have them. Send them, okay?"

Colleen snorted. Apart for more than a year and Amy still called about missing items? Really, one would think she could afford to buy a new CD or two. The afternoon phone call from New Mexico probably cost as much as the damn collection. She wondered how Amy was getting along with Gertrude. Colleen laughed out loud. She'd never pictured Amy with someone named Gertrude. Not Trudy, Gertrude. Colleen tried to imagine saying "Oh, Gertrude!" in the heat of passion. It just didn't work.

Beep. "Hi, darling. This is your mother. I know you told me you can't check on the house next week, but I was hoping you'd change your mind. I talked to William and he will be so busy. Call when you get home. By the way, don't forget Andrea's birthday. I sent her twenty dollars. Meagan will complain, but a child can never learn the value of money too soon. Dad sends his love."

Beep. "Col? This is Lisa. Sorry I was such a jerk. Just jealous. I'm real happy you're going to Rehoboth. Honest. See you at work. Oh, and by the way, I didn't tell Janis. She's such a gossip. 'Bye."

Colleen grimaced as she got up and went into her tiny kitchen to feed Smokey. What a boring social life, she thought. The only phone calls she got were from her family or ex-lover or co-worker? She'd never even had anyone over for dinner.

She left the kitchen area and stripped off her work clothes. Catching a glimpse of herself in the full-length mirror on the back of the closet door, she stopped in critical assessment. In the white lace satin bra and underwear she didn't look too bad. Her body was soft and curvy; ample breasts filled out the sexy bra. Across skin that was almost as white as the undergarments, beige freckles scattered like thrown confetti. Her red-gold hair contrasted sharply with ice-blue eyes in a not unpleasant way, she thought, her golden lashes darkened subtly with brown mascara. Her nose was okay, not too big or too small. Lips were a bit too thin by Kate Moss standards, but their color was naturally rosy. She thought her legs were too short, but they had a nice shape. Trim ankles, delicate feet. And wild hair — the humidity had turned it into a jumble of unruly curls. She'd often considered cutting it, but Amy had always objected. Well, Amy was in New Mexico with a new lover named Gertrude. Perhaps the time was right to take the bull by the horns and just do it.

After changing into a pair of jeans and an old Melissa Etheridge T-shirt, she walked barefoot to the kitchen and grabbed a can of Arizona iced tea. Flipping to the country-western station on the radio, she picked up the *Blade* and flopped onto the couch. When Smokey finally settled into her lap, she tried to read, but the cat had other ideas. He constantly tried to maneuver his body onto the paper and, when that didn't work, bit and clawed the edges. Colleen gave up and opened the travel book. Rehoboth had a couple of accommodations specifically for women, but she wouldn't mind staying someplace with gay men too.

At the first lesbian B&B she phoned, Sand in My Shoes, it sounded like a party was going on in the background. "You want a room at the beach two days from now?" the woman yelled into the phone. "No problem. And I suppose you want Martina as a roommate too?"

Colleen was taken aback, then realized the woman was joking. "Guess that's asking a lot, eh?"

"Keep trying, honey. You might get lucky with another B&B."

"Thanks." Colleen hung up and dialed the next place on her list.

"Paper Nautilus, this is Suzanne," the gravelly voice on the other end answered.

"Hi, yeah," Colleen said. "I was wondering if you had any rooms starting this weekend and going for about two weeks."

"You're in luck, hon. Just got a cancellation not thirty minutes ago." Colleen heard the sound of pages flipping. "Might have to change rooms next weekend, but I think I can accommodate you for two weeks. Is this for two or one?"

"Just one. It's a business trip. I should be done in two weeks, maybe less."

"Good. Booked solid after that. By the way, if you don't stay the full two weeks, I'll still have to charge you unless I get someone to fill in."

"That should be okay." Colleen gave her name and got directions to the place. "You take American Express?"

Suzanne laughed heartily. "Sure do. As the boys in town say, 'The American Express card, don't be a homo without it.' "

After she hung up, Colleen couldn't believe her luck — first an assignment to the beach and then finding a lesbian bed and breakfast with an available room. She pulled the Emerson file from her briefcase and began reading Candy's will. Brian's gossip intrigued her. She'd had a gut feeling that the dead woman was "family," and the will pretty much confirmed it. Candy had left her entire estate to various gay, lesbian, and AIDS organizations. That fact made Lori Kestler all the more interesting. Was she a bodybuilder too? Could she lift a 245-pound barbell to someone's neck?

Colleen took notes as she read and reread the files, jotting down the names of people she needed to talk to, questions she wanted to ask. Should she come clean with people about why she was in Rehoboth or should she try an undercover-type approach and feign morbid curiosity? The answer was clear before she'd even finished asking herself the question. She hated to lie and was a terrible actress. She couldn't even stand doing role-plays in school. She decided to feel out the people and then choose which tactic would give her more truthful answers.

Yawning, she examined the newspaper photos one more time. "Steroids?" she asked Smokey as she scratched his ears. Amy had once dragged her to see a bargain matinee of *Pumping Iron: The Women.* Didn't seem possible for either men or women to get so muscular without help from something. Probably a phony tan too.

She leaned back and closed her eyes. She tried to imagine what it would be like to make love with someone so muscular and so strong. She wasn't really attracted to blondes so she tried to recall some of the other women she'd seen in the movie. One stood out in particular — couldn't remember her name, but she had had an Australian accent. Yes, she was very strong and definitely not blonde.

* * * * *

Backstage after the competition, the contestants were milling about, their pumped up, tanned bodies glistening with oil. Some had already dressed, but a couple were still wearing their skimpy posing suits. Colleen stood in the doorway of the dressing room and watched the rippled bodies. One woman was brushing her hair, another used a towel to wipe the oil off her long legs. They seemed to be moving in slow motion, every gesture, every movement exaggerated. Her eyes searched the room until she found the one she'd come to see — the cute one with the foreign accent.

She approached shyly. The woman looked at her and smiled. "Well, hello there," she said in a husky voice. "You came in just to see me, didn't you?"

Colleen blushed. "Yes. Yes, I did. How did you know?"

"I noticed you in the audience. You have the most beautiful blue eyes, but I bet all the girls tell you that."

Suddenly, they were alone in the room, and it was no longer the dressing room. Somehow they'd wound up at the bodybuilder's hotel. She was divesting Colleen of her clothes. Her mouth seared kisses over her shoulders and neck. Those strong, muscular arms picked her up and carried her to the bed. The lean body pushed Colleen into the feather pillows. She kissed Colleen deeply; her long fingernails raked across Colleen's thighs. Long fingernails?

* * * * *

Colleen yelped in pain as Smokey's claws dug into her jeaned leg. Someone pounding on her door had startled him. He jumped off her lap as she groaned both in pain and disappointment. "Such a nice fantasy," she grumbled under her breath, and then yelled, "Who is it?"

"It's the pussy patrol," a muffled voice answered.

She got off the couch and opened the door. Brian leaned against the wall, holding a bulging plastic bag. "What were you doing?" he asked as he pushed past her and strolled into the room. "I've been knocking for days."

"I was, uh, busy. Didn't hear you is all."

"Didn't hear me? Maybe you should get the noise level on your vibrator checked. Or buy a Miracle Ear." He smirked.

She wrinkled her nose at him. "Very funny. You want something to drink?"

"I'll take a beer if you have one. I got some magazines at the gym for you. I found an old one with a feature article on that muscle dyke who was killed. Cotton Candy."

Frowning, she handed him a Corona Light. "Emerson. Candy Emerson."

"Whatever." He collapsed onto the couch, barely missing Smokey. He turned the plastic bag upside down and several glossy magazines spilled out. They all had bulky men on the covers. He picked one up. "I should start reading these," he said with a gleam in his eye. "These guys are a little too big for me though. Their muscles, I mean. Can't imagine them being too big where it counts."

"You're such a lecher," Colleen replied affec-

31

tionately. She instructed him on the care and feeding of Smokey, then picked up one of the magazines. "It was really sweet of you to get these for me. Which one has the article on Candy?"

"The one with the beefy blonde. Page twenty-nine. She was quite something. Won the Ms. Olympic Universe title three times. Numerous endorsements. No mention of any boyfriend."

"Did it say anything about her gym in Rehoboth?"

He chugged his beer. "Just mentioned that she owned one. It's mostly a review of her career. Retired four years ago. It did mention a partner though. Some guy. Maybe she swings both ways, eh?"

Colleen ignored him and flipped through the pages of the magazine.

"So," he said, "you find a place to stay yet?"

"Sure did. I'm staying at the Paper Nautilus on Baltimore Avenue."

"What a lucky break! Some of the best gay places are there. Lambda Rising, the Blue Moon restaurant, the Dream Café. You'll meet tons of available women without even leaving the block. Oh, and there's a cool store around the corner called Splash."

"Brian," she said, exasperated, "I am going down there to work, not to cruise."

"All work and no play makes Colleen a bitchy queen. Don't you think it's time you spread your . . ." He paused suggestively.

"Brian!"

". . . your wings, Miss Gutter Mind, your wings."

Colleen had to laugh.

"You know," he continued, "when you finally give up the celibate life you're gonna be like a sailor on leave. Believe me, I know."

Colleen grinned. "How would *you*, of all people, know anything about the celibate life?"

"Not celibacy, honey. Sailors on leave is what I know about." He put his beer bottle on the table with a loud thunk. "Gotta go. Thanks for the beer." He kissed her on the lips, patted Smokey's head, and waltzed to the door with dramatic flair. He paused before he closed the door and turned back to add, "Call me when you get laid!"

Colleen threw a book at the door, but he was already laughing his way down the hall.

After she'd showered and brushed her teeth, Colleen pulled out the bed couch and settled under the fuzzy blanket. She read the article on Candy Emerson's career, then thumbed through the rest of the bodybuilding magazines. Her mind filled with images of strong women, she turned off the light, hoping to pick up her fantasy where she'd left off . . .

CHAPTER 3

The rain was beating down so hard that Colleen could barely see the car in front of her. Wasn't it just her luck — she gets a free trip to the beach and it pours. If this mess kept up, it would take her double the time to drive to Rehoboth.

Brake lights glowed like cat's eyes in the wet gloom ahead. The driver in front of her piloted his car erratically, riding the brakes and drifting over the dividing lines, sometimes right and sometimes left. Colleen tried to change lanes, but the other car kept drifting. Her nerves were on edge as she saw the Chesapeake Bay Bridge looming in the distance. Without signaling, the car in front of her switched lanes and took the last right turn before the bridge.

"Good riddance, you pinhead!" Colleen yelled at his disappearing tail lights.

After she'd crossed the long expanse of the bridge she breathed a sigh of relief. The rain stopped almost as quickly as it had started, and she made it to Rehoboth only forty minutes later than she had planned. The sky was clear and the sun burned hotly.

She drove slowly down Rehoboth Avenue, taking in the atmosphere and making mental notes of the interesting looking shops. The sidewalks were jammed with gaggles of giggling teenage girls, swaggering groups of teenage boys, parents with children, and of course the gay men and women who had turned Rehoboth Beach into their own Atlantic paradise. She couldn't wait to join them.

At last she found the Paper Nautilus. The hot air blasted her as soon as she got out of the car, but she was dressed for the weather in deep purple shorts with matching top. Her hair she'd put up in a ponytail. She extracted a heavy suitcase, her brief-case, and a cosmetics case from the trunk and hauled them to the open front door. From the small, enclosed porch, a black Cocker Spaniel greeted her with tail wagging.

An attractive, older woman followed the dog. She extended her hand. "Hi. I'm Suzanne and this is Shadow. You must be Colleen. Welcome to the Paper Nautilus."

"Thanks so much." Colleen shook her hand, then bent to pet the dog. "I can't believe how lucky I am to get a room here on such short notice."

"Yes. We've had a very busy summer. I believe you said you were coming on business? How did you find the Paper Nautilus?"

Colleen straightened up. The dog padded back into what looked like the living room and hopped up onto a sloping blue chair. "In one of those travel books," she answered, stretching her arms and shoulders after the long drive. "And yes, I'm here on business. Couldn't ask for a better place to be assigned." Suzanne seemed trustworthy so she made a split-second decision. "I work for an insurance investigation agency, and I'm here to check into the death of Candy Emerson."

Suzanne's demeanor changed immediately. The friendly welcome in her blue eyes was exchanged for one of hostile suspicion. "I thought that case was settled."

Colleen instantly regretted her candor. "The insurance agency has some questions. It's just routine."

"They don't want to pay out because she was gay, do they?"

"Was she? That never came up in any of my discussions." She cringed inwardly at her white lie.

"Isn't that why they sent you? Thinking you could blend in with the community and dig up dirt?" Suzanne narrowed her eyes. "You're not even gay, are you?"

"Yes. Yes, I am. I'm not here as a spy. Really."

Suzanne didn't answer right away, just stood staring at Colleen with a frown knitting her brow.

Colleen felt uneasy under the scrutiny and shifted her weight uncertainly. Even the dog seemed to be eyeing her with suspicion.

"Look," Colleen began, "if you don't want me here . . ."

Suzanne relaxed and smiled again, but the welcoming glint did not quite return to her eyes. "No. You can stay. I apologize for my reaction. Let me show you to your room. Be careful, the stairs are steep."

She grabbed Colleen's suitcase and led the way. The hallway at the top was not much wider than the stairs, but it was bright with sunshine from the many windows lining the wall. Pale mauve carpeting muffled their footsteps. On the doors were hand-lettered signs — "Calico Clam," "Pink Conch," "Thorny Oyster," "Lightning Whelk." At the end of the hall, Suzanne stopped at the "China Moon."

"This is one of the larger rooms," she said as she unlocked the door. "I thought you'd be more comfortable here because you'll be in town for so long."

"It's great. Thanks."

"Hope it's not too noisy for you. An after-hours dance club is right behind us."

"A dance club?"

"Yes, it's a gay club and restaurant. They might not be open much longer, though. They've been having financial trouble because they can't get a liquor license. Some of the locals don't like the idea of having a gay bar in the middle of town. In fact, Candy was trying to work with the city council about changing that. She was well-respected, no matter what you might hear."

Colleen sat down on the double bed. Suzanne remained standing, her arms crossed and her stance defensive. "Suzanne, listen," Colleen said, "I'm really not here as an enemy. Candy had a double indemnity on her policy. It's standard practice to investigate this type of claim." She decided to take another chance. "And if this was murder, it may be that one of her beneficiaries was involved. Wouldn't you want the truth to come out?"

Suzanne relaxed her stance, but her voice was accusatory. "You think Stephan had something to do with it?"

"I don't think anything yet. And she had another beneficiary as well."

"I can't imagine who. She wasn't involved with anyone, although she had started dating again."

"What about Lori Kestler?"

Suzanne curled her lip. "That bitch? She and Candy were together until about eight months before Candy died. Never could understand the attraction. Anyway, Lori's gone straight. Not that I ever thought she was really gay. I think she just liked Candy's money and celebrity status." Her eyes widened in surprise. "Don't tell me Lori is a beneficiary too!"

"Well, yes."

Seemingly overcome with disbelief, Suzanne sat down on the bed. "Candy felt that much for her? They were only together about a year." Her gray eyes sparkled with anger. "There's your suspect. Lori and that homophobic jerk she's with now."

"I'm sure the police questioned them."

"Ha!" Suzanne deepened her voice. " 'Were you at the gym the morning in question? No? Okay, you can go now.' *That* would be the extent of their questions."

"You've had trouble with the police? They don't respond to complaints from the gay community?"

Suzanne jumped up off the bed. "I've already talked too much and I have things to do. Continental breakfast from seven to eight-thirty on the porch. Enjoy your stay." She closed the door behind her.

Alone in the room, Colleen felt a bit overwhelmed. The long drive had drained her energy and left her knotted with tension. And the excitement of being in Rehoboth for the first time, coupled with the stress of her first solo investigation, made her feel dizzy. She stretched out on the bed and stared at the slowly rotating ceiling fan. In the quiet, she was suddenly aware that the room's air conditioner was off, but the room was surprisingly cool. She could feel her body relaxing. She toyed with the idea of getting Candy's file from her briefcase, but decided instead to mentally review what she knew.

She wanted to skip over the gruesome details of Candy's death, but some of her earlier questions now had possible answers, as well as additional questions. Lori Kestler had a definite motive. Candy could have taken her off the policy at any time. But why didn't she do it after the breakup? Perhaps Lori and Candy had had an argument about the policy? And now there was another suspect. Lori's boyfriend, the homophobe. If Lori wasn't capable of lifting 245 pounds, perhaps he was. In her mind, strangling someone with a barbell seemed more like a man's method than a woman's. A sexist assumption, she knew.

Post-mortem put Candy's death at about an hour before Stephan Gray allegedly discovered the body. Why wouldn't an experienced bodybuilder like Candy have waited for her workout partner before doing heavy lifts? Colleen knew from reading the magazines Brian had brought her that such a partner — a spotter — was like a piece of equipment. Perhaps Candy did have a partner that morning? Why assume that she didn't? Did she work out with someone regularly? Stephan claimed to have found her dead when he arrived to open the gym at six-thirty that morning. Did Candy usually work out before then? Could she have stayed late the night before? And why did Stephen need to turn on the lights when he arrived? If Candy had been working out alone, who had turned them off?

None of these questions were answered in the police report Mr. Sampson had given her. She needed to get a copy of the autopsy results, but Suzanne's comments made her wonder just how cooperative the local authorities would be. If they wanted to ignore or cover up a possible murder, they wouldn't appreciate her snooping around.

Colleen glanced at the clock. It was still relatively early. She decided to go into town and get a feel for what was around. As she unpacked her suitcase, she remembered that she still needed to buy a bathing suit. She slipped her wallet into a pocket and put on a pair of oversized sunglasses. She locked her door and headed down the hall. The house was very quiet. She assumed the guests were still out sunbathing. Shadow greeted her as she came down the stairs, but Suzanne was nowhere to be seen.

As she ventured outside, a beautiful house with

blue paint and pink awnings immediately caught her eye. A sign showed it was the Blue Moon that Brian had mentioned and her travel book listed as a restaurant and bar. Several men were gathered on the outside terrace. Colleen looked at her watch. Four o'clock. Happy hour had just started. As she headed toward the Blue Moon, she caught a glimpse of a rainbow-painted fence. It lined a short passageway that led right to Lambda Rising's Rehoboth bookstore. She decided to check it out.

Tables and chairs were set up along the fence. The two women sitting there looked like they'd walked right off the cover of *Deneuve* magazine. They were eating delicious-looking cakes and sipping tall drinks. She smiled at them and they smiled back. Rehoboth is a great place, she thought as she entered the store.

A salesclerk with short, spiked hair the color of sweet butter greeted her enthusiastically. "Hey, how ya doing? Enjoying the sun?"

Colleen smiled back. "Just arrived. Haven't had a chance to be out in the sun yet. It's great to be here though. My first time."

"Really? Well, welcome! My name's Bianca. Where are you staying?"

"Across the street at the Paper Nautilus."

"Great! Vera and Suzanne are wonderful. Here on vacation, I assume?"

Colleen nervously fingered the postcards at the counter. "Actually, I'm here on business. I'm checking into the accidental death of Candy Emerson." She watched carefully for Bianca's reaction.

"It's about time someone checked into that. Some of us never believed it was an accident."

"Some of who?"

Bianca shrugged. "You know, some in the community. Candy had one or two enemies here. We've had a rash of gay bashings too. Vandalism of gay businesses. Could just be random violence I suppose, but the gym was locked from the inside. Had to be someone who was already there."

"Are these theories, or do you know something? Have you talked to the police?"

Bianca came from around the counter and lit a cigarette. She took a deep drag and motioned for Colleen to follow her outside. She sat down and propped her feet up on the table. "The police had no reason to talk to me officially. Besides, they only wanted to solve the case quickly and quietly." Colleen looked at her quizzically. "The tourists come here to escape from big city crime and violence. Murder's bad for business."

Colleen sat down next to her. "It does seem like an odd accident. I mean, Candy was a professional. She knew the dangers of working out alone with heavy weights like that."

"Yeah, she knew, but Stephan — that's her business partner — was always getting irritated with her because she wouldn't always wait for him. He spotted for her in the mornings."

"Is Stephan a bodybuilder too?"

"Not professional like Candy was. They've been friends forever — can't remember how they met. I'm sure someone told me once. I think he was a bodybuilding groupie. You know, someone who hangs out at all the competitions."

"Can you think of any reason why he'd want her

dead?" Remembering how Suzanne had reacted when asked about Stephan, Colleen felt she might be on shaky ground with that question, but Bianca answered calmly.

"Can't think why. He was really devastated by her death."

"Could he have been in love with her, or something like that?"

Bianca laughed. "Well, they did love each other — like sisters. Stephan's as gay as they come."

"He does gain financially," Colleen pointed out.

Bianca thought a minute and then said, "I know Phillip's medical bills must be pretty high. He's been in and out of hospitals and treatment centers for God knows how long. But I never got the impression they needed money."

"Phillip is Stephan's lover?"

Bianca stubbed out her cigarette and leaned back in her chair. "Yeah. Poor guy. He's got AIDS. Stephan sent him to Mexico a few months back for some experimental live cell treatment."

Bianca stood up as an adorable troupe of baby dykes entered the store.

"I'll let you get back to work," Colleen said. "How do I get to the gym from here?"

"Turn left when you get to the street and keep going until you reach the boardwalk. Turn left and walk all the way down to Virginia Avenue. The gym is right on the boardwalk. Stephan usually closes up around six. Probably pretty empty. Happy hour, you know."

"Thanks, Bianca. Can I come back if I have more questions?"

Bianca waved from the doorway. "Sure. You can come back even if you don't. Have a good time, and say hi to the Paper Nautilus girls for me."

Feeling thirsty, Colleen stopped in at the small dessert café right next to the bookstore and bought an iced tea. The young man who served her was as friendly as Bianca, and she marveled at the difference between Rehoboth's friendly atmosphere and the big city attitude she was used to.

As she passed the Blue Moon, she noticed that the crowd had gotten larger and louder. The men were gorgeous, with picture-perfect bodies and well-groomed hair. It looked like a *GQ* convention.

The streets were crowded. People still in bathing suits dragged chairs and umbrellas and kids back from the beach; others were already dressed for a casual evening out. The boardwalk was even more jampacked, but as she headed toward the north end, the crowds thinned. She passed by a monstrous hotel that looked like a huge pink gingerbread house, then a large antique shop, and suddenly she found herself sharing the boardwalk with nothing but seagulls. The arcades, the stores, all gone. It was peaceful and quiet, like standing behind the roar of a waterfall.

She saw the gym, its unobtrusive sign painted onto the large plate glass window in block letters: Bodies By the Beach. Silhouettes of male and female bodybuilders posed beneath the words. In the lower left corner of the glass, a translucent rainbow triangle discreetly identified the business as gay-owned or gay-friendly. Colleen felt the tension mount in her body as she gazed in through the window. It was creepy to think of what had happened inside. Even if Candy Emerson's death did turn out to be an accident, it still gave her an uneasy feeling. She could see maybe five people inside the gym, all of whom appeared to be male. She took a deep breath and opened the door.

CHAPTER 4

Colleen was wrong. Three of the five people in the gym were women, women with broad shoulders and large, muscular arms. One, wearing a bulky sweatsuit, was doing bicep curls; the other two worked together on some strange-looking piece of equipment. One of the men rode a stationary bike, and the other appeared to be checking records of some kind on a clipboard. The man on the bike was the only one who looked like he needed to be in the gym. The rest looked so fit and trim that they seemed poured out of a perfect mold. Colleen felt dumpy in her baggy shorts and loose-fitting top. Her shoes were bargain-basement, Keds-type sneakers, not the utilitarian but fashionable Nikes or Reeboks or whatever was the brand of the day.

The man with the clipboard set down his papers and approached her. He was tall, with a perfectly sculpted body and a deep bronze tan. His coal-black hair was a hair-dresser's dream — thick and wavy, with just a hint of gray at the temples. Dark eyes hinted at a deep sadness despite the welcoming smile that revealed even teeth starkly white against his tan. She wondered if they were naturally perfect or if he'd gotten a little help from the dentist. His nose was just a bit too large, and a faded scar ran along his cheek from ear to chin.

"Hi," he greeted in a deep baritone. "Welcome to Bodies By the Beach. My name is Stephan Gray." They shook hands. "I'm the owner, and I'll be glad to answer any questions. Can I show you around?" He made a sweeping gesture.

"Thanks. Colleen Fitzgerald. I'm only here for a couple of weeks and I've never even stepped foot inside a gym before."

He took her arm and propelled her to another strange-looking contraption. "You've come to the right place. We've got state-of-the-art Nautilus equipment, all brand new. We can design a special workout program just for you. We also have daily aerobic classes. Twice a week we have yoga. Do you exercise at all?"

"Well, I walk a few blocks to and from the subway everyday."

"That's a start. Some people come in here and tell me they literally do nothing. What do you think you're more interested in? Weight training? Aerobics?" He led her into another room. "This is where we have our classes. New mirrors and flooring. It's more private. No tourists ogling you through the front window."

"Do you get many gawkers?"

His eyes seemed to darken further, as if a curtain had fallen over them. "Not until recently. We had an accident here a few months back. Just morbid curiosity-seekers. The novelty will wear off."

"Yes, I heard about Candy Emerson. Tragic. You were close?"

"Very. We were much more than business partners. She was a good friend and I owe her a lot. She helped me out of a nasty situation. Got me off of a reliance on steroids. She was adamantly opposed to them. Tried to keep them out of this gym, but it's fighting a losing battle."

"She never used them herself when she was in competition?"

He looked at her sharply. "You're not a reporter or anything, are you?"

"No, not a reporter." She took out her wallet and showed him her ID. "I'm an investigator with Sampson and Rhoades. We specialize in insurance cases. Fidelity Life and Casualty has hired us to check out a few loose ends concerning Candy's death."

"Let's go into my office," he said curtly as he turned his back to her and returned to the main room. She followed him with a sinking feeling in her stomach. It hadn't been her intent to make him angry. He entered a small cubicle that barely held a desk, a file cabinet, and two chairs. He gestured to the chair in front of the desk.

"Mr. Gray," she began, "I didn't mean to offend you."

"So, what reason do they have for not wanting to pay?" he interrupted. "The police investigated. They said it was an accident. What more does Fidelity need?"

"This is purely routine with policies as large as this one." The purely routine excuse was beginning to wear on her nerves, but she knew those words would come out of her mouth many more times before this investigation was finished. "We just need to be absolutely sure that no foul play was involved."

"What, you think someone killed her?"

"You're not the only beneficiary."

He laughed harshly. "You think Lori Kestler is capable of murder? She must weigh all of ninety-five pounds. No way could she lift that barbell and —" He stopped and didn't finish.

"Why was Candy here alone? Was this a usual practice for her?"

He ran his hand through his hair before he answered. "I have asked myself that question over and over. Sure, she worked out alone, but never when she lifted heavy. She knew better than to lift that amount of weight without a spotter. She should have waited for me."

"You told the police you turned the lights on when you opened the gym that morning?"

"Right. That's when I saw —" He stopped and took a deep breath.

"I'm sorry. This is very indelicate, I know. If

Candy had been working out all alone, why weren't the lights on when you arrived?"

"The lights? Oh, we have two sets of lights, the regular overhead daytime lights and then the softer night lights. Candy always preferred the night lights."

So much for that theory, she thought. "Did Candy have a workout partner?"

"Me, and sometimes Gillian."

"Gillian?"

"Yeah, Gillian Smith. She's our aerobics instructor. Sometimes she and Candy worked out together, but never when Candy did heavy lifting. I was the only one Candy trusted to spot her."

"Do you think someone might have been hiding in the gym overnight, waiting for Candy to come back?"

"No. I closed up the gym the night before and I always check everywhere — locker rooms, sauna, steamrooms. No one was here when I left."

"Could Candy have come to the gym with someone that morning, or maybe met someone?"

"Anything's possible, I guess." Stephan sighed.

"What about Lori Kestler's new boyfriend? Some people have hinted that this was an anti-gay hate crime, and I hear he's a real homophobe."

He looked at her in surprise. "You've really been around, haven't you?"

She ignored the question, preferring to let him believe she knew more than she was letting on. "Have there been a lot of bias crimes here? Did Candy have any enemies? Maybe somebody had a grudge?"

"She angered some of the townspeople by her support of the after-hours club over on Rehoboth

Avenue, but a contested liquor license doesn't seem a good enough reason to kill someone. She didn't flaunt being gay. When she first came here, people were happy to have a celebrity in their midst. They even considered hosting an official bodybuilding competition."

"What about the steroid issue? You said she tried to keep them out of the gym. Did she have trouble with someone in particular?"

Stephan played with the papers on his desk. He seemed reluctant to answer. Colleen waited patiently. She didn't want to risk losing his cooperation. His hostility seemed to have evaporated.

"I don't like to accuse people without firm proof, but we do have one client that Candy was pretty sure was dealing. She couldn't get anyone to admit that they bought the steroids from him, but she knew the signs. In answer to your earlier question, Candy did use them herself, a long time ago. More an experimentation. She stopped before she entered the professional ranks."

"This guy, could Candy have had a confrontation with him?"

"She was *always* having it out with him. One time he almost hit her."

"Did you call the police?"

"There's no law against *almost* hitting someone."

"Why did you let him stay a member of the gym?"

He threw up his hands. "Do you know how many times we asked ourselves that same question? But the law won't let you throw out a paid-up member unless you've got really good grounds. We couldn't risk a discrimination suit, so we decided to just keep an eye on him. Kept hoping he'd slip up and we'd catch him selling."

"What's his name? Does he live in town?"

"The guy's name is Barry Charles. Big, hulking guy with shoulder-length blonde hair and bad skin. Typical of steroid use — the bad skin I mean." Stephan looked at his watch and stood up. "Look, I'm sorry, but it's almost closing. I've got to start cleaning up."

"Are you really satisfied that this was an accident?"

"Who the hell cares what I think? It won't bring Candy back and it sure as hell won't make the insurance company any more eager to pay up."

"Believe me, I am not out to get you, Stephan, but if Candy was murdered, wouldn't you want the killer caught?"

"Look, I've finally accepted her death and the ruling. Why dredge everything up again?"

Stephan stood and she followed him into the empty weight room. The silence seemed ominous. She shook her head to rid herself of such melodramatic thoughts. She glanced at the four benches lining the right wall and a shiver ran up her spine. Which one had Candy been using, she asked herself. She tried to imagine a scene — Candy trying to lift the heavy weight off of her. Was there an assailant looming above her, indifferent to her struggles? Wait a minute! Candy was strong. She lifted these weights all the time. Why wouldn't she have been able to do so then? She opened her mouth to ask Stephan, but the dejected stoop to his broad shoulders made her decide to wait. She'd opened enough old wounds for the day.

She held out her hand. "I'm sorry to have caused you any pain," she said. "I hope you understand my position. Can we talk again later?"

He took her hand. "Sure. And listen, come back and I'll design a program for you. Free use of the gym while you're here."

"Thanks."

He left her standing in the middle of the room. As she turned to go, a woman exited the dressing room. She was the one who had been doing bicep curls when Colleen arrived. Her tanned skin was the color of dark honey; her warm brown hair with the golden tips was cut short. Thick but nicely shaped brows arced over wide, almond-shaped eyes of dark forest green. Her nose was thin, the nostrils slightly flaring, and her mouth was generous, made for kissing. Her posture was perfectly straight, her shoulders wide, hips narrow. She had changed out of her sweats and now wore tight bicycle shorts and the inevitable tank top. Colleen preferred this new outfit, which allowed her to more easily admire the woman's tall, muscled body. She certainly has a nice backside, Colleen thought as she watched her go out the door. What a sexist thing to say, her mental PC guardian chided. Give me a break, the lonely side of her argued back, it's been months since I've been with a woman.

"I wonder who she is," she said out loud.

"Who?"

Colleen jumped. "Stephan! You startled me. I didn't hear you come out."

"Sorry." He grinned sheepishly. "Now, who did you see?"

"Cute, brown-haired woman in bicycle shorts. She was in the gym when I first arrived."

Stephan smiled. "Oh, that was Gillian Smith, our aerobics instructor. Used to be a professional competitor, one of the best in the country."

"Really, she doesn't seem bulky enough to be a bodybuilder."

He gave a hearty laugh. "You're letting your stereotypes show. Not all bodybuilders look like those beefy guys you see on the magazine covers. But anyway, Gillian was an aerobics competitor."

She nodded. She'd seen those things on ESPN. Lots of sweaty bodies jumping around to loud music. Seemed kind of trivial to her, but then, most sporting events left her cold, except for figure skating. She didn't know a double axel from a triple lutz, but she could watch Katarina Witt for hours.

She left the gym and started walking back up the boardwalk. Stephan stuck his head out the door and yelled to her, "Hey Colleen! Gillian teaches every morning at ten. Come on by tomorrow for class."

Smiling, she waved to him, then continued toward the Paper Nautilus. She felt like getting a drink and relaxing a little, but where to go? She considered the Blue Moon, but it was packed with men. The women must go somewhere. When she got back to the B&B, two women were leaving. The dark-haired one was slightly taller than the blonde. Evenly tanned, she was thin with a boyish figure. Her short hair was elaborately styled so that it stood straight up and ended with a curl over her forehead. Her brown eyes were warm and friendly. The blonde's sun-bleached hair was longer, curling gently at the shoulders. Bangs emphasized eyes a deeper blue than Colleen's own. She was tanned too, but not as darkly as her companion. They both wore khaki shorts, white T-shirts, and Dockers without socks.

Colleen stopped them. "Say, do you know where the women go around here?"

"Square One restaurant over on Wilmington Avenue," the dark-haired one answered. "We're on the way there. Wanna come?"

"I'd like that, but should I change first?"

"Nah, you look fine. My name's Denise and this is my lover, Jenny."

"Colleen. Just arrived today from D.C."

The three of them headed up the street. Colleen was glad she'd run into Denise and Jenny; she would never have found the place on her own. They stopped in front of a white stucco building that looked more like a house than a restaurant. The "place to be" was the large patio in the back.

Denise was right. This was where the women gathered. They had to fight their way to the bar through a throng of lesbians in various stages of dress. A few were still in bathing suits; one was in a thong bikini. Colleen stopped momentarily to admire the tight buns. Embarrassed, she turned away and followed Jenny and Denise. Brian must be more right about me than I realize, she thought.

Denise shouted her order above the music and conversation to a blonde bartender who looked liked Tasha Yar on *Star Trek: The Next Generation.* "Hey Daphne, give me a draft and a white zinfandel." She turned to Colleen. "What are you drinking?"

"Oh, just a 7UP with a twist of lime."

"And 7UP with lime."

Denise tapped on the bar in time to the music. Jenny excused herself to go to the ladies room. It gave Colleen a chance to look around; she wondered if she might see someone she knew from D.C. Her gaze lingered on one or two of the women, including Denise. She tried to notice which ones seemed more athletic, figuring they might be members of the gym and therefore potential sources of information. If she were a little more honest with herself, she'd admit that her glances had nothing to do with business. She was attracted to these androgynous women, who were as different from her past lovers as they could be. Even Amy, who played softball, had been extremely feminine. And pretty. Warm brown shoulder-length hair with red highlights. Pale blue eyes that matched Colleen's own; freckles too. Medium height and thin. Breasts on the small side, but she looked great in a muscle T. But Colleen had always had a vague sense of discontent with her relationships, and she wondered now if it was because her lovers were too much like herself. Lipstick lez. Femme. What were the labels used these days?

Jenny returned at the same time that her lover brought their drinks. Denise waved away Colleen's offer to pay. The music and loud voices precluded any kind of conversation, allowing Colleen to continue scanning the bar. A ripple ran through the crowd as someone came through the double doors and walked down the stairs. It seemed as if a sea of faces all turned to see who entered. Colleen smiled with pleasure — it was the woman from the gym. She had changed into tight, black jeans and a pale green polo shirt.

"Hey, Gillian," someone called out, "haven't seen you in a while. How's it going?"

"Hi, Jane," she answered in a deep voice that made Colleen feel tingly all over. Gillian was then enfolded into the crowd, but her tall form made it easy to see her.

Colleen turned to Denise and leaned close. "Do you know that woman?"

"Yeah, that's Gillian Smith. She's pretty popular around here. Could you tell? Teaches aerobics at the local gym. Kind of keeps to herself though."

"Any particular reason?"

"Believe me, lots of women have tried to find out. She really took it hard when Candy Emerson died." Probably assuming that Colleen was unfamiliar with the local scene she added, "Candy was this body-builder who owned the gym where Gillian works. People suspect Gillian and Candy were lovers, but no one knows for sure."

Colleen raised her eyebrows at this new piece of information. It didn't make her very happy. "This seems like a small community," she said. "Isn't it pretty obvious who's dating who?"

Denise shrugged. "No one ever saw them out together as a couple. I guess people just picked up vibes when they saw them at the gym. A look here, a casual touch there. Anyway, Candy was crushed to death under a barbell one morning. Speculation shot through the roof after the accident."

"Speculation about whether it was an accident?"

Jenny interrupted. "Denise, you shouldn't dredge up old gossip. The issue is settled, whether we're happy about it or not."

Denise drained her beer. "Guess you're right. Ready for another drink?"

"Thanks, no," Colleen said. "Any chance that you could introduce me to her?"

"Impossible," Denise replied. "That group she's with won't let her go all evening. I'll give you a hint though. She likes to walk along the beach late at night. No specific time. Be back in a sec." Denise headed back to the bathroom.

Colleen soon tired of the noise, and the crush of bodies made it terribly hot, even out on the patio. She tapped Jenny on the shoulder. "I think I'm going to head out. It's too crowded for me. I'm hungry too. Thanks for the drink."

As she fought her way through the crowd, Colleen glanced to where Gillian stood surrounded by her admirers. Suddenly, Gillian looked up and stared right at her. The look was like a caress. Colleen felt a tremor run through her body. She lowered her eyes. Surely she was mistaken? She glanced up again. Gillian still stared at her, but this time with a cocky smile. Colleen's face burned. She could only smile briefly and hurry away.

Back at the Paper Nautilus, she stood out front for a moment. Although the night air had gotten a little cooler, Colleen still felt hot. Her reaction to Gillian was unlike anything she had ever experienced before. Not even Amy, her most long-term relationship, had evoked such feelings in her. She opened the door and walked in.

"Are you okay?" Suzanne asked with some

concern. "You look all flushed. Maybe you were out in the sun too long for your first day?"

Colleen patted her cheeks. "Oh no, I didn't even go out on the beach today. I spent some time with Bianca at the bookstore — she says hi by the way — then went to the gym. Had a long talk with Stephan."

A short woman with dark curly hair entered the room. Shadow followed close on her heels.

"This is my lover, Vera," Suzanne said. Vera put out her hand and smiled. "Colleen is here to investigate Candy's death for the insurance company."

Vera stopped smiling and let go of Colleen's hand. "What? You guys don't want to pay up so you're here to drag this thing out as long as you can, looking for things that aren't there?"

Suzanne spoke soothingly. "We had a long talk, honey. It's not anything like that. Just routine stuff. And if she finds out the truth, wouldn't that be great? Her being here could be a blessing in disguise."

"Yeah? Well, you tell Stephan that."

Colleen tried to reassure her. "I promise I'm doing all I can to make sure this is resolved as soon as possible."

Vera still wasn't smiling. "Well, we'll just have to see. I'd better get dinner ready." She left without a backward glance.

"You'll have to excuse Vera. After the murder, all the publicity leeches came crawling into town asking questions. Low-life reporters offering big money for any dirt on Candy. Everyone's been pretty tight-lipped though. Got to protect our own."

"I understand." Colleen had noted Suzanne's

reference to murder and was about to question her further when Vera's "Honey, can you come help me with this?" rang out from the kitchen.

"Can you recommend a good place for dinner?" she asked instead.

"Sure, there's lots of good places. Depends on how much you want to spend. There's a diner right on Rehoboth Avenue that's gay friendly. Food is good, and inexpensive. Or Mano's on Wilmington. It costs more, but has great food and atmosphere." She reached under the coffee table and pulled out a bunch of menus. "Here, check these out and see what suits your fancy.

"Thanks." Suzanne turned to leave. "Uh, one more thing," Colleen said, "do you know Gillian Smith? She teaches at the gym."

"I know her through her relationship with Candy. We would get together every so often. She's kept mostly to herself since Candy died."

"Were they lovers?"

"That's my guess. But Candy was still getting over Lori, and I think she was taking things very slow. I assumed she and Gillian were dating, but whether it went beyond that I don't know."

"Any chance you could introduce me?"

"I don't think she'll talk to you about Candy."

"That's not why I want to meet her," Colleen answered and felt the rush of blood to her face again.

Understanding seemed to dawn in Suzanne's eyes. "Oh yes, of course." She stood silent for a moment, then said, "Sorry, I wouldn't feel comfortable introducing you two — your being an investigator and all . . ."

"Of course. Sorry."

The disappointment in Colleen's voice must have been obvious. "I have to warn you, Colleen, I don't think she's over Candy yet. It's only been a few months."

"Uh, thanks. See you later," Colleen called as Suzanne walked back into the kitchen. Colleen couldn't believe she was so transparent. She only hoped that when she did meet Gillian, she wouldn't make a fool of herself the way she just did.

CHAPTER 5

Waking up the next morning, Colleen couldn't believe it was only Friday. The summer sun streamed in through her window. It was hard to think of having to work on such a beautiful day, but she forced herself out of bed and took a quick shower. None of the other house guests were up and about. She maneuvered her way down the narrow staircase and into the living room. Someone had set out coffee, hot water for tea, and several different kinds of pastries. She grabbed a mug of coffee and a piece of cranberry bread and sat in the high-backed chair near the front window. She sipped the coffee; it had a slight cinnamon flavor. She looked up as a young African-American woman entered the room. She was very short and dressed casually in red shorts and a navy-blue bikini top.

"Hi there. My name is Colleen."

"How ya doing? I'm Amanda. Have to leave today unfortunately. Just came for a couple of days so I could study for mid-terms. Need to go back so I can use the university library this weekend."

Colleen was puzzled. "Mid-terms?"

"Summer school," Amanda replied as she took a slice of lemon cake. "I'm in law school at Virginia Tech."

"Do you come here often?"

"Every chance I get. I love being here with all the queers. Thinking of setting up a law practice here one day."

Colleen took a sip of her coffee. "Do you know a lot of the residential crowd?"

"Some. I hang out at Bodies — that's the local gym — so I mostly know those people."

"Did you know Candy Emerson?"

Amanda let out a long sigh. "Not as well as I would have liked, if you know what I mean. Talk about a major babe!" Then she laughed. "I kidded myself into thinking I could help her get over her ex, but she gave those honors to her aerobics instructor."

"Were there hard feelings over the breakup?"

"Well, Lori hurt Candy pretty bad. Her name is bad news around here. The community was pretty protective of Candy, her being a celebrity and all. And she was a great person — really helped out whoever needed it. Lori was just out for a good time.

Everyone knew it. Everyone but Candy, that is. When they broke up, we all expected a Martina–Judy type of situation, but Lori didn't ask for any money."

"Maybe that's because she knew she was the beneficiary on Candy's life insurance policy."

The incredulous look on Amanda's face was almost comical. "You're not serious? Lori benefits from Candy's death? Whoa!"

"Did Lori have any problems with money that you know of?"

Amanda eyed her suspiciously. "You're some kind of cop or something, aren't you?"

Colleen carefully wiped the crumbs off her fingers. She stood and refilled her coffee before answering. "I'm on your side," Colleen reassured her. "I work for an investigative firm hired by Candy's insurance company. They just want to make certain that Candy's death really was an accident." She watched Amanda carefully to see if her initial friendliness would turn hostile. "I could use your help if you have any information you think might be important."

Amanda relaxed. "I don't think I'm around enough really to be of any help. You need to talk to her business partner, Stephan, or the aerobics instructor, Gillian Smith."

"I've already talked to Stephan, but I haven't met Gillian yet. Do you know her well enough to give me an introduction?"

"No. You need to talk to Vera or Suzanne for that. Gillian keeps to herself. Very private. No one is even one hundred percent sure she and Candy were lovers, but that's the general consensus." She looked at her watch. "Well, sorry to eat and run, but I've got to get going. Maybe I'll see you around. Good luck."

Colleen was sorry to see her go. She would have bet that Amanda could give her more information than she realized. She sighed. As far as good sources went, all fingers pointed in Gillian's direction. She decided to take the morning aerobics class Stephan had suggested.

Colleen couldn't remember the last time she had exercised, especially in a group situation. She had an old pair of sweat pants, and she could wear an oversized T-shirt. It was only 8:30. She wondered where Vera and Suzanne were.

As if they had read her thoughts, both women materialized. Suzanne's smile was a bit more friendly than Vera's. "How'd you sleep last night?" Suzanne asked.

"Great. I didn't even need the air conditioner." Colleen helped herself to another piece of bread. "This cranberry bread is excellent. Who's the baker?"

Vera lifted the lid off the coffee pot and peered in. She nodded and put the lid back on before turning to face Colleen. "We usually order our baked goods from the Dream Café up the street here, but I decided to try my hand yesterday. Glad you like it."

"So," Suzanne said, "did you get much information?"

"No. I'm going to the police station today to check out the official reports. Then I'll need to talk with Stephan again ..."

Vera gave her a nasty look. Suzanne patted her lover's arm. "Don't get so upset, honey. I told you the kid was okay."

65

Colleen smiled, hoping to soothe Vera's concern. "I'm not out to defile Candy's name or to find some loophole so the insurance company won't have to pay Stephan. Please believe that. I only want the truth, and some people don't seem satisfied with the police explanation. Are you?"

Vera stared at her, then turned on her heel and marched into the back of the house.

Suzanne patted Colleen's shoulder. "Everything will be fine. When you go to the station, ask for Officer Perry. He's a friend of ours."

Colleen was baffled. She couldn't decide if they wanted to find out the truth or not. They seemed to want to accept the accident theory even though they didn't believe it.

The phone started ringing and Suzanne rushed to answer it. "Paper Nautilus . . . Yeah, sure." She held the phone out to Colleen. "It's for you."

"Hello, this is Colleen."

"This is the sex police calling," came the familiar voice.

"Hello, Brian."

"I was just wondering, when you stay at a lesbian bed and breakfast, do they give you a lesbian for your bed or for your breakfast, or is it both?"

"You are a sick man, Brian, and I've got to get down to business."

"That's what I've been telling you for months."

Colleen ignored the innuendo. "I've got to go, Brian."

"Smokey and I have bonded, and everything is okay. *Ciao!* "

Colleen hung up the phone, giving thanks that Brian worked weekends so he couldn't come tease her in person. The phone book sat on the table, and she snatched it up. No Kestler, Lori or L. Unlisted, or not in Rehoboth? She flipped the pages. Pay dirt this time. Charles, Barry. Felton Street. She took a map from the stack and headed upstairs to change.

The sky blazed an electric blue, dotted with wisps of dandelion clouds. The sun flashed in citrine splendor. Colleen could feel her skin already prickling from the heat. Her sweat pants suddenly seemed incongruous. What had she been thinking of? She knew. She wanted to hide her less-than-perfect body from Gillian.

At Bodies By the Beach, she pushed open the door and was treated to a cool rush of air. The gym was noisy with the sounds of chains and pulleys and weights. She glanced around and saw a bunch of big hairy men lifting heavy weights. As they grunted and growled their way through their workouts, she was reminded of the great apes enclosure at the National Zoo.

A couple of anorexic-looking gym bunnies in body-hugging leotards and thongs bounced past her into the aerobics room. Colleen looked down at her baggy sweats and felt like a total geek. Then she spied a woman doing sit-ups on a mat in the corner. Dressed in sensible shorts and a T-shirt and a little on the heavy side, she made Colleen feel like a normal person again.

Stephan came out of his office, clipboard in hand. He broke into a smile when he saw her. "Colleen. How are you today? You look ready to work out."

She nervously tugged at her hair. "Thought I'd try the aerobics class this morning."

"Good idea. Now, don't feel bad if you can't keep up. Just do what you can. We always have people of differing levels take the class. You can put your bag in the women's locker room."

"Thanks," she said to his retreating back. He approached a thin man who struggled with some kind of calf-building machine. "You've got too much weight on here," she heard him say. "Let me help you."

She went into the locker room and almost rushed out again. A completely naked woman was drying her hair in front of the mirror above the sinks. Colleen felt extremely self-conscious, but couldn't help but glance admiringly at the woman several times. She quickly stuffed her knapsack into a locker and left.

In the aerobics room, several people were warming up, so engrossed in what they were doing that no one looked at her. Glad of that, she started to stretch. After a few minutes, she heard a bit of commotion. She straightened up as Gillian walked into the room and stepped onto a raised platform. Her lithe, muscular body was dressed in black spandex shorts and a cream leotard that showed off her honey brown tan. And those incredible green eyes! They made Colleen want to drown in their depths. Gillian set down a cassette player, inserted a tape, and turned toward the class. Was it Colleen's imagination, or did Gillian's eyes flick over her in recognition? And something else? A slow song that Colleen had never heard began to play.

"Okay, class," Gillian said in a deep authoritative voice, "let's begin. We'll start with some stretches."

At the end of the hour, Colleen felt as if she'd

tumbled down a steep incline. She figured that's how she looked too. Her hair had come loose from its ponytail; she could feel it curling wildly around her face. She tried to surreptitiously wipe the sweat from her forehead using the collar of her T-shirt. She'd managed to keep up with the class, but she knew she'd regret it later. Later? She regretted it now. The cool-down portion of the class hadn't done much to cool her down. She lay back on the mat and closed her eyes. As she concentrated on keeping her breathing even, she became aware of someone looming above her. She opened her eyes slowly. Gillian stood grinning above her.

"You didn't do too bad for a beginner," said the husky voice. "You're going to be sore tomorrow though. I can recommend some good ointment and some stretches that will help."

"Thanks." Colleen was horrified to hear her voice squeak. She coughed to clear her throat. "You're such a good teacher, it wasn't hard to be inspired." Her cheeks burned with embarrassment. Did she really say that?

Gillian grinned. "I like when I affect my students that way. Say, didn't I see you at Square One last night?"

Colleen sat up, and Gillian reached out a hand to help her stand. She took Gillian's hand and froze as the touch sent an electric jolt up her spine. Gillian's dark green eyes glowed with an unnamed emotion. Colleen stood awkwardly and gazed back into Gillian's eyes, unable to look away. She was surprised at her own boldness.

Gillian reached out a hand and brushed aside a curl of hair that fell over Colleen's forehead. "I haven't seen anyone with red hair like yours in a long time. It's lovely. What's your name?"

"Colleen Fitzgerald," she whispered.

Gillian kept staring at her, then said brusquely, "I have to go now." She turned away.

"Wait!" she called.

"Yes?" Gillian kept her distance.

"I'd like to talk to you. Away from here. Please."

Gillian relaxed her shoulders. "Okay. Wanna meet at the diner on Rehoboth Avenue around one?"

"Thank you." Colleen smiled up at her.

Gillian grinned slyly. "And just what would you like to talk about?"

"Candy Emerson, for one thing."

Gillian looked taken aback. "You and I have nothing to talk about."

CHAPTER 6

Colleen watched Gillian walk rapidly out of the room. She felt incredibly stupid. She shouldn't have mentioned Candy's name so soon. How was she going to break through that wall with which Gillian surrounded herself? She didn't want to talk to Gillian just because of the case. She had felt something between them, and she was sure Gillian had felt it too. Well, she would come to aerobics every day until Gillian relented, even if it killed her.

She winced as she rolled the mat up and put it on the stack with the others. Every inch of her body screamed with pain. She walked gingerly out of the room, taking small steps to avoid any jarring of her overworked muscles. Stephan spotted her in the doorway. He came over immediately, his eyebrows knitted in sympathy.

"Didn't take my advice, I see. My prescription is a hot bath and lots of aspirin, and no aerobics tomorrow."

"I didn't want to embarrass myself," she moaned in reply. "Guess I did that anyway."

"You'll be fine," he soothed. "The walk back to Paper Nautilus will do you good."

"I can't go back there right away. I need to go to the police station, then to Felton Street. I also want to find Gillian somehow and apologize."

"Two questions. What do you want on Felton, and why do you have to apologize to Gillian?"

She put her hand at the small of her back. "I want to talk to that Barry Charles fellow."

"You stay away from him! He's dangerous, and he won't help you."

"I want to find out what kind of guy he is."

"Believe me, if he thinks someone is trying to pin something on him, watch out. Stay away from him."

"If he's that bad, why haven't you done something about him? He still comes to this gym, for crying out loud."

"Colleen, I told you before — it's less of a hassle to let him continue coming here than to try and keep him out."

"Have you gone to the police?"

Stephan laughed harshly. "They don't care. We gave them Charles' name as a possible suspect in the latest gay bashing, but they didn't even question him." He looked straight at her. "You're out of your league. The best thing for you to do is just go back to your cushy little job in the big city and leave us alone."

"I think you want me to leave because you have something to hide," she accused.

Two spots of red appeared on his cheeks. "Of course I don't. What could I have to hide?"

"How about a sick lover in Mexico? I imagine his treatment isn't cheap."

Stephan seemed flustered. "Yes, Phillip's in Mexico, but that has nothing to do with this. I am not engaging in illegal activities!"

"It does give you a motive. And you had the opportunity. Candy trusted you to spot her when she lifted heavy." As soon as she said it, Colleen regretted it. She certainly didn't believe it. She waited for Stephan's anger.

He merely sighed and shook his head. "The police already checked that angle. When Candy died, I was at the police station reporting a stolen car. Check for yourself."

"I'm sorry, it wasn't in the police report." She paused, feeling guilty. "Listen, I'm going to talk to Barry Charles. If it will make you feel better, I'll try to do it when other people are around. Okay?"

"Guess I can't stop you. Now, I have to get back to my clients."

At the police station, a receptionist told Colleen that all available officers were attending in-service training, so she headed toward Felton Street. She had no trouble finding Barry Charles' place. Badly in need of a paint job, the two-story house sat a stone's throw from the sidewalk. A dead tree stood a lonely vigil to the left, and patches of dried grass spotted a lawn that had not been mowed in quite a while. The windows were curtainless, but the top-floor windows appeared to have green shades of some kind. The driveway was empty, but someone had obviously done an oil change recently. The whole place gave Colleen the willies. As she watched the house, she got the feeling that she, in turn, was being watched. Thinking it would be better to talk to Barry Charles in a more public place, she decided she'd have someone at the gym point him out to her next time he came in.

As she walked away, Colleen kept glancing over her shoulder. She couldn't shake the feeling that she was being watched. One time she swore she saw a face at one of the lower-level windows, but when she looked more intently she saw nothing. It was with relief that she found herself back on Rehoboth Avenue. She decided to eat at the diner. The place was busy. She had to wait for a table, and she made sure to get a booth just in case Gillian did show. As she perused the menu, she told herself to quit dreaming. She had angered Gillian somehow. Somehow? She knew exactly what she had done. Some investigator she was turning out to be.

A handsome young man with the ubiquitous perfect tan came to take her order. "Ready yet?"

"Yes, just give me a grilled cheese and french fries. And a Coke. No, make that an iced tea. With lemon."

"Sure thing," he said with a flip of his long blonde hair.

"That's a real healthy meal," a deep voice said. She started. Gillian grinned at her. "Mind if I sit down?" Without waiting for an answer, she slid into the opposite seat.

"I didn't think you were coming," Colleen said.

Gillian shrugged. "I didn't either, but Stephan told me all about you. If someone did kill Candy and you help nail him, then I'm on your side. I don't want any personal questions though."

"I have to ask some." She noted that Gillian too wasn't totally convinced that Candy's death was an accident.

"No, you don't. Candy and I were good friends. That's all you need to know. And I had no reason to kill her, so don't give me that look."

The waiter brought Colleen's iced tea. "Hey, Gillian," he said with genuine warmth. "It's been a while. You having your usual?"

"Not today, Dimitri. Just bring me an iced tea too."

Colleen added three packs of sugar to her tea. She ignored the look Gillian gave her. "I'm interested in your theories about who might have wanted Candy Emerson dead. I'd like to know more about Lori Kestler and her boyfriend."

"Believe me, that guy doesn't like queers and thinks they should all get the hell out of town. You know the gay dance club next to the diner?"

"Yeah, Suzanne told me they've been having trouble getting a liquor license."

"Yeah, well you should have heard some of the

75

things he said about gay people at the public hearings. And the disgusting things he said to Candy. I think it drove him crazy that his girlfriend had been with a woman."

"And Lori?"

"Well, she and Candy were together about a year. I have no reason to suspect her of anything, but I guess for some people a million-plus dollars is reason enough to kill. But Lori? She's a tiny little thing, could never have done it alone. Can't weigh more than ninety-five pounds. Never could understand what Candy saw in her."

"This boyfriend. Is he big enough?"

"Oh sure. He's a big hulking thing. Steroids."

"I couldn't find a listing for Lori Kestler in the phone book. Does she live here?"

"She lives with him. Phone could be in his name. Albert Simmons out on Josephine Street, beyond Silver Lake. They've got quite a nice spread. Lori freelances for one of those bodybuilder magazines. That's how she and Candy met."

Dimitri brought Gillian's iced tea and Colleen's lunch. Somehow it didn't seem quite so appetizing now that Gillian was watching her. She wondered what Gillian's "usual" was. Probably sprouts and tofu, she thought somewhat cynically.

"Maybe I should have a salad with this," Colleen said.

"Wouldn't hurt. I'll have one too." Gillian motioned for Dimitri to return. "We'll have two house salads. Low-fat Italian." She turned her attention to Colleen again. "So, Stephan tells me you went to visit Barry Charles. You're here in one piece, so I assume the meeting went well."

"I didn't see him. I found the house, but I didn't go in. It gave me the creeps."

"Probably best. He's a pretty scary guy. Candy hated having him around the gym, but she hoped to catch him dealing. She wanted the police to help, but they weren't interested unless she had proof."

"Sounds like the police have been uncooperative in a lot of things."

"Guess I'm not being fair. The police aren't so bad. They just have their hands full in the summer with all the tourists. Some of us in the community were disappointed in their verdict about Candy's death because we didn't think they had done enough digging. But there really was no evidence otherwise."

"What about this Officer Perry that Vera and Suzanne know?"

"David, that's Officer Perry, is a good guy. His cousin Bianca is gay . . ."

"Bianca at Lambda Rising?"

"Yeah, you've met her?"

"Yes, she seems really nice."

"She's the best," Gillian agreed. "So anyway, he watches out for her at Lambda Rising and keeps his eye on the other gay businesses."

Colleen sipped her iced tea. "Why aren't you convinced that Candy's death was an accident?"

"Something's just not right about this whole thing. It's just a feeling I have." She paused, then shook her head. "But how could she have been murdered that way? I mean, how could someone just sneak up behind you and drop a huge barbell on your neck?"

"What if it was someone she trusted? Someone who was working out with her that morning — spotting for her while she did heavy lifts?"

"Possible, but not probable. The only person Gillian trusted to spot her when she lifted heavy was Stephan." Gillian looked at Colleen defiantly. "And he didn't do it!"

"What if someone forced her to lie on the bench, say at gunpoint?"

Gillian thought a moment. "That would take at least two people. There's no way you can hold a gun and a two hundred and forty-five pound barbell. And I don't believe Candy would just lie there. She would have gone out fighting." She sighed deeply and put her head in her hands.

"Gillian, I'm so sorry . . ."

Gillian looked up. "I don't know, Colleen. Maybe it was an accident. Candy knew the dangers in working out alone, but she always did it anyway. Maybe she ran out of second chances."

Colleen reached across the table and put her hand over Gillian's. The pain in Gillian's voice made Colleen want to take her in her arms. Instead, she said, "I'm really sorry. I know you and Candy were close."

"She was a terrific person. So talented. So strong. Do you know how hard it is to win the Ms. Olympic Universe title? Candy did it three times in a row. She was so strong and so beautiful. I could easily have loved her."

"Didn't you?"

Gillian toyed with the straw in her iced tea. She

left her other hand resting under Colleen's. "No. I wouldn't let myself. I knew it couldn't last. I was a diversion for her. She was still in love with Lori. Deep inside, she really thought that Lori would come back to her."

The two women were silent. Their food went uneaten. Gillian absently sipped her iced tea. Their touching hands remained motionless. Colleen was afraid to break the spell.

"Well, well, isn't this a cozy little scene?" Dimitri's voice shattered the stillness. "Are you two girls gonna eat your food, or what?"

Colleen snatched her hand away. She felt like a little girl caught doing something she shouldn't. Gillian frowned at him. "Just give us the check. And don't go thinking something."

He placed the check on the table with flourish. "The girls will be disappointed, Gillian. You know you're the hottest catch in town." Dimitri turned to Colleen, "I hope you know karate, honey, 'cause you're gonna have to fight off a lot of women if you wanna keep this one." He parodied a martial arts demonstration, complete with sound effects.

"I don't know why you insist on spreading gossip," Gillian retorted. "You're such a drama queen!"

"If the crown fits ..." He tossed his long mane of blonde hair and sashayed to the kitchen, singing "Everybody was Kung Fu fighting ..."

Colleen was surprised to see Gillian smiling. "You're not angry with him?"

"He only does it to get my goat. I'll get him back next time."

Before Colleen could pull out her wallet, Gillian

threw down some money, grabbed her hand, and pulled her out of the booth. "Come on, let's go for a walk."

"Can we stop by Paper Nautilus and drop off my knapsack first?"

Gillian led Colleen through Rehoboth Mews, a small shopping alley next to the diner, and on toward the Paper Nautilus. "I thought I'd take you to meet Lori Kestler. Why don't you change into your most business-like attire?"

"Sure. It'll just me take a few minutes."

"I'll wait for you at Lambda Rising," Gillian said as she crossed the street.

Colleen entered the house and dashed up the narrow stairs. She quickly showered and then put on a pale gray linen skirt and white cotton blouse. Sampson and Rhoades liked its agents to wear jackets whenever interviewing clients, but it was much too hot out. She even decided to forgo pantyhose, hoping her black flats wouldn't give her blisters. She brushed her unruly hair into some semblance of a French braid and put on her pearl earrings and some pale pink lip gloss. She surveyed herself in the mirror. What would Gillian think? It suddenly mattered very much.

Colleen's shoes were already sticky and she could feel them rubbing against her heels as she entered the bookstore. Bianca and Gillian were laughing.

"Ah, there you are," Gillian said as she turned

toward the door. Colleen was satisfied to see admiration light up her eyes. "I like your hair that way."

"Do you think I look professional enough?" Colleen asked as she twirled around.

"Yes, but it's a long walk. Would you prefer to drive?"

Bianca threw her keys at Gillian. "Here. Take my car. It's right out front."

They got into a bright green Toyota Celica adorned with rainbow flag and lambda bumper stickers. Gillian drove and Colleen stared out the window. She liked Rehoboth's charming, tree-lined streets and turn-of-the-century architecture intermingled with more modern abodes. Past Silver Lake, the houses took on a much wealthier look.

On Josephine Street, Gillian parked in front of a large two-story house. Its paint job reminded Colleen of Grey Poupon mustard, and the roof shimmered a deep cobalt blue. A large bay window was filled with a jungle of hanging plants, and more plants lined every inch of the catwalk that surrounded the entire house. The wide expanse of lawn, bisected down the middle by a brick-lined walkway to the front door, was obviously watered daily. The expensive Kentucky blue grass was afforded the right amount of shade by the two large oak trees that stretched majestically overhead. Colleen could see the tops of more trees behind the house. Two cars were parked on the street right out front — a Mercedes and a Jaguar. Colleen didn't see anything that could pass as a garage.

"Albert Simmons must make an awful lot of money to afford a place like this," Colleen commented. "What does he do for a living?"

"He's into a lot of things. Has some rental property, stuff like that. He also owns a gym in Ocean City, but it's a real pit. The phone may be in his name, but the house belongs to Lori. I suspect that Candy bought it for her. She was very generous." A look of pain crossed Gillian's face. Colleen took her hand and they sat in silence for a moment. "So," Gillian asked, "how long do you need? Shall I come back in about an hour?"

Colleen looked at Gillian in surprise. "You're not coming in with me?"

"You'll do just fine on your own. Besides, Albert doesn't like me much. Neither does Lori actually. So, I'd rather not."

Colleen got out of the car. She leaned one elbow on the door and stuck her head back in. "Thanks for driving me. I don't know how long I'll be, so you just go on and I'll make my own way back into town."

"Are you sure?"

"Yeah, I'll be fine. Catch you later?"

Gillian switched on the ignition. "Sure, as long as we don't talk business."

Colleen stepped back and watched her drive away. She certainly hoped to see Gillian later. And she had no intention of talking business. In fact, she hoped they wouldn't do much talking at all. She squared her shoulders, marched up the walk, and rang the bell. The door opened immediately and a petite woman stood silently before her.

Colleen extended her hand. "Hello. My name is Colleen Fitzgerald and I represent the firm of Sampson and Rhoades. I'm investigating the death of Candy Emerson. Are you Lori Kestler?"

The woman ignored the identification that Colleen offered. "I know who you are," she answered with an edge to her voice. "Word gets around."

Colleen dropped her hand. "May I come in?"

The woman stepped back. "Don't suppose it could hurt. Follow me."

She led Colleen through an antiques-filled living room and into a modern kitchen with a large window above the sink. Sunlight glinted off of the brand new pale yellow cabinets and dazzling white appliances. The white and yellow floor was as shiny and slick as an ice rink. The woman motioned Colleen to sit at an oak table in the corner.

"You want something to drink?"

"Iced tea would be great."

As the woman busied herself at the sink, Colleen used the opportunity to examine the person she assumed was Lori Kestler. She was a far cry from Gillian Smith. Where Gillian was tall with broad shoulders and slender hips, Lori was petite and small-boned with curvy hips accentuated by spandex shorts. Lori's pale flaxen hair was so fine and cropped so close to her head that she appeared almost bald. Her skin was whiter than Colleen's own, something Colleen didn't ever think possible. With her pale lashes and luminescent colorless eyes, she didn't seem alive. She reminded Colleen of a porcelain doll she'd owned once, fragile and delicate and no fun to play with.

The tea kettle whistled, and Lori poured hot water into a glass filled with ice cubes. Lori dunked a tea bag into the water once or twice and then discarded it. She splashed some lemon juice into the pale liquid and plunked the glass down on the table.

CHAPTER 7

Colleen sipped the tea. As she expected, it tasted pretty awful, but she wasn't about to tell Lori that. She smiled in what she hoped was a pleasant way. "I assume you're Lori Kestler."

"Good assumption." Lori remained standing in front of the sink with her arms crossed.

This is really going to be fun, Colleen thought. "I don't mean to pry, but you and Candy Emerson had an intimate relationship?"

"Yes."

"Did you know that Candy Emerson had named

you and Stephan Gray as co-beneficiaries on her life insurance policy?"

"Yes."

Colleen took another sip of her tea. Lori's stance remained unchanged. She obviously had no intention of making this easy. "I've been told that your new boyfriend threatened Candy."

"Who told you that? That bitch, Gillian Smith?"

"Look, Ms. Kestler, I know this isn't easy for you, but it's not easy for me either. My firm sent me to investigate Candy's death. It's just routine, but to be honest, Fidelity is somewhat suspicious of the accidental death ruling."

"Yeah, right." Lori sneered. "Isn't it funny how insurance companies always get suspicious whenever it's their turn to pay up?" Colleen made no reply. "Look, I don't know why you would think Albert or I had anything to do with this. I certainly can't lift such a weight, and Albert was here with me anyway. We're each other's alibi. So why don't you tell your damn insurance company to stop being so cheap and just pay up."

"I'm sure that's what will happen as soon as I turn in my report." Colleen tried a new tactic. "Do you know of anyone else who might have wanted to kill Candy. Any run-ins with townspeople? Old enemies?"

Lori uncrossed her arms and started pacing. "We've been through all this with the police. Didn't you read their report?"

"Yes, but it wasn't too helpful."

"Well, I think you should question that partner of hers. He's got a good motive, if you ask me. That lover of his dying in Mexico, despite expensive treatment. They've got their house mortgaged to the hilt and Stephan flies to Mexico every chance he gets. That can't be cheap. Check his bank account. Bet it's empty."

Colleen didn't want to believe Stephan capable of murdering his good friend, but love or desperation was a strong motive. Just how far would he go to help Phillip? She made a note on her pad to double check his alibi. Lori spoke up again.

"Oh yes, there's also Robbie Taylor. They were fierce rivals during Candy's bodybuilding days. They absolutely hated each other."

Colleen was perplexed. "What do you mean by 'hated each other'?"

"You've got to understand that the bodybuilding circuit can be pretty ruthless — some people will do anything to get ahead. Sabotage, blackmail, you name it."

"So what happened with Robbie Taylor?"

"It was the day before the finals of the Ms. Olympic Universe contest. Candy had won the title two years in a row, but this time the smart money was on Robbie. She looked incredible." Lori's eyes glowed at the recollection. "Cut to shreds. Absolutely ripped. There was no way Candy could touch her." Lori moistened her lips with her tongue.

"And then . . ." Colleen prompted.

"And then, she quit."

"She quit?"

"Yup. Quit the contest and quit bodybuilding. Candy won, of course, and the buzz on the circuit was that she had found out something about Robbie that she threatened to go public with."

Colleen was intrigued. No one else had spoken of

Candy except in the most glowing terms. Could she have been that devious, that ruthless? Colleen wondered if Lori was making something up to throw her off the trail. No one she'd talked to had even mentioned this Robbie Taylor person.

"Do you know what the secret was?" she asked.

Lori stopped her pacing for just a moment as she gazed out the window. "I don't know why I should tell you."

"You cared about Candy once, and she obviously cared about you. If she was murdered, wouldn't you want to know who did it?"

"Look, you'd better be leaving soon. Albert will be home in a little while and I don't want him to see you. He's very jealous."

"Why would he be jealous of me?"

"He doesn't like me to be alone with women."

Hmmm, Colleen thought. This was interesting. Could Albert have seen Lori and Candy together and gone ballistic? As much as she disliked Lori, she didn't want to risk her safety if she had a boyfriend prone to violence.

"What does Albert do for a living?" Colleen asked in what she hoped was a casual way.

"Different things. He's part-owner of a gym in Ocean City. He's also been in a few local competitions. Won some money that way. That's how we met. I was covering one of the competitions for my magazine."

"Isn't that how you met Candy too?"

For a brief moment Lori's face softened. It made her seem vulnerable. Then she frowned. "I don't want to talk about myself. Do you want to know Robbie's secret or not?"

Colleen smiled. "Of course. What is it?"

Lori leaned forward conspiratorially. She dropped her voice to a melodramatic whisper. "She used to be a he."

Colleen couldn't help but laugh out loud. "You expect me to believe that?" She stood up.

Lori leaned back against the sink and crossed her arms. "Okay. Don't believe me. I don't care. I'll still get the money, no matter what. You better leave now."

"Thanks for your time. I'll show myself out."

She exited into the scalding heat, instantly regretting her modified business attire. As she began walking in the direction she hoped was correct, her feet seemed to expand with every step. She could tell this was going to be blister city. She chided herself for not calling a cab from Lori's house.

She had walked about six blocks when she heard someone honking at her. She ignored it at first, thinking it was some man being a smartass. Then she thought she heard her name. She looked at the car. It was Stephan!

"Colleen!" he called out. "What are you doing out this way? Do you need a ride back?"

She quickly approached the car. "Stephan, you're a life saver. I'd love a ride."

He leaned over and unlocked the passenger door. She got in and kicked off her shoes. He reached into a grocery bag and pulled out a bottle of Deer Park spring water. "Here, you look like you could use this."

She took a long drink and leaned back into the seat. "What are you doing out this way?"

"I had to go out to the offices of *The Whale,* our

local paper. I'm putting in an ad for the gym. We need to get some more permanent members. The summer crowd just isn't enough when you've got year-round bills."

"You're not afraid of getting the wrong kind of clientele?"

Stephan laughed. "Straight people, you mean? Hey, heteros aren't all bad. Why, some of my best friends are straight, Hell, my parents are straight, Phillip's parents are straight . . ."

Colleen laughed back a bit self-consciously. "Sorry, I didn't mean to be so blatantly heterophobic."

"Well, you're not the first gay person to ask me that, but business is business. I let potential members know that Bodies is a gay-friendly business. If they don't want to join because of that, then I don't want them anyway. Now, what were *you* doing out here?" He glanced over her attire. "You look like you had business to take care of."

"Yes, I was interviewing Lori Kestler."

"Oh. That must have been a thrill."

"She wasn't very friendly, if that's what you mean." Colleen paused. "She did tell me something very interesting though."

"Some kinky sex secret? How to be a total bitch in three easy lessons?"

She ignored his sarcasm. "What do you know about a woman named Robbie Taylor?"

"She was one of Candy's main rivals during her professional life. Why?"

"Lori said Robbie has a dark secret that Candy was going to expose. Hinted that it might relate to Candy's death."

Stephan snorted. "Candy's been out of competitive

bodybuilding for almost five years. I doubt she's even had any contact with the old crowd. If she was going to expose some secret, it would have been during the competition."

"Right. That's what I mean, Lori said it was during Candy's final Ms. Olympic Universe contest that she found out."

"Found out what?"

"That Robbie used to be a man."

Stephan glanced at her incredulously. "Lori told you that? And you believed her?"

"No, of course I didn't believe her," Colleen said defensively. Then she paused. "Okay, to tell you the truth, I don't know what to think. I'm grasping at straws here, Stephan, and I'm no closer to the truth than I was before I came here."

Stephan patted her knee reassuringly. "You're doing just fine. You've only been here two days. What do you expect? You know that all of us suspects are going to do whatever we can to throw you off the path to the truth."

Colleen looked at him. He had such a handsome profile. He was every man's dream, or every woman's, for that matter. Straight woman, that is. But his dark eyes always had that hint of sadness. Even now as he joked with her, his smile never quite reached his eyes.

"Stephan," she said, and took a deep breath, "just how ill is Phillip?"

His profile hardened. He gripped the steering wheel. "He's dying. The doctors give him another four months at the most. No amount of money will save his life, Colleen." He turned to her and his voice broke. "I did not kill Candy Emerson."

91

Colleen recoiled from his intense stare. He drew in a deep breath that sounded like a sob, then looked back at the road. They were almost to Rehoboth Avenue. She saw the tears in his eyes and felt like a total jerk. "I'm so sorry. I believe you. Please, please forgive me."

He looked beaten. "Nothing to forgive. It's just been so hard for me. Phillip and I have been together for almost twelve years. I still can't believe I'm going to lose him. You don't know how often I've wanted to bring him home."

"Why don't you? If they can't help him, why leave him in Mexico?"

Stephan looked desperate. "I'm afraid that if I ask him to come back he'll think I've given up hope." He pulled up in front of the Paper Nautilus, turned off the ignition, and put his head in his hands.

Colleen touched his arm. "Have you asked Phillip how he feels about coming home? Maybe he wants to be with the man he loves and who loves him. I know that's what I would want. What if he's afraid to come home because he thinks he'll be a burden on you? What if he's only staying away because he doesn't want *you* to lose hope? Maybe you should ask him if he wants to come home."

"I've wanted to so much, but I'm afraid. How will I know how to take care of him? I can't stand to see him in pain."

She took his hand. "There are lots of people who would help you. You're not in this alone."

They sat in silence for a long time. Stephan took his hand from hers and leaned over to kiss her cheek. "Thanks. I'll think about what you've said."

As Colleen stepped out of the car he added, "And listen, don't pay attention to Lori Kestler. She just likes to stir up trouble."

Colleen was starving. No wonder, she thought, considering what she and Gillian had *not* eaten for lunch. Gillian. How could she have let her go without making a date or at least getting her phone number? She didn't even know where the woman lived. She doubted that Vera or Suzanne would give out the number — they seemed to be very protective.

As she entered the Paper Nautilus, Shadow started barking. His tail was wagging so hard, Colleen thought he'd tip over. "How ya doin' fella?" she asked as she scratched his ears. She straightened up to find Vera standing in the doorway to the private part of the house. She was drying her hands on a dish towel. Colleen smiled and was happy to get a return smile.

"Did you have a good day?" Vera asked. "Looks like you've been to work."

"I just had an interview. Didn't think shorts would be appropriate." Colleen began her ascent to the top floor. She stopped midway. "Do you mind if I use the phone when I come down?"

"That's what it's there for. No long-distance calls, though, unless you use a credit card or call collect."

Colleen continued up the stairs and down the hall to her room. The ceiling fan had once again done its job; her room was cool despite the heat outside. She stripped off her clothes and threw them in the corner. Putting on a white sundress and matching sandals, she headed back downstairs. She stopped at the phone and checked through the phone book. No

Gillian Smith. Not even a G. Smith. She sighed. Rehoboth Beach on a Friday night, and she was all alone. It was the story of her life.

The diner was crowded, mostly with families with young children. She decided to sit at the counter. Dimitri came over as soon as she sat down.

"Back again so soon," he stated. "Can't get enough of this great food, eh?"

She laughed. "I like it just fine. I'm surprised to see you're still here. What time do you get off?"

He looked at his watch. "In about five minutes. Then I'm heading over to the Blue Moon to start the weekend. You got plans?"

"I'd hoped to, but no luck this time."

"Gillian give you the slip?"

Colleen blushed. "Just give me an iced tea, will you?"

"Coming up!" he said. He plunked the glass down in front of her. "You could hang out at Square One, but I don't think Gillian will go there tonight. A moonlight walk along the beach? Now, that might be a good idea. The tea is on me." He untied his apron and disappeared into the kitchen.

As she sipped her tea, Colleen took her notepad out of her purse and wrote her notes for the day. Accident or murder? If it was an accident, she had to gather enough information to show Fidelity that she had checked everything thoroughly. And, if it was murder ... What a coup, Colleen thought, if she could solve a murder case on her first assignment. Well, one way or the other, she had to come up with something soon. She was sure that Kevin Sampson was using this case as a test. If she couldn't cut it, would she be out the door?

She tapped her pencil on the paper. She had no evidence that this was a murder, nor did the police. So why was half the gay community so certain that it was?

A group of rowdy dykes strutted into the diner and piled into a booth. The pleasant distraction reminded Colleen that Rehoboth offered other things to do besides work. She closed her notebook and decided to buy some suntan lotion and a bathing suit. Splash, the store Brian had mentioned, looked promising. Maybe she'd rent a bicycle and cruise around town. Dimitri's replacement came over and she ordered the special.

By the time Colleen left the diner, night had fallen. The streets were still filled with people. The stores would not close for some time. After about an hour of wandering in and out of the shops, she headed over to Square One. The music was loud, the crowd equally so. She worked her way to the bar.

"Seven-Up with lime," she shouted above the din. The same woman from last night was bartending. What was her name? Daphne? Colleen took her drink and surveyed the room. Lots of cute women here tonight, she thought, but her mind pictured only Gillian. Was it only last night that she'd seen Gillian here? A twinge in her muscles reminded her that it was only this morning that she'd taken the aerobics class. Lost in her thoughts, it took a few moments for her to realize that someone was at her elbow.

"Where were you?" Denise asked. "I've been talking to you for five minutes."

Colleen smiled. "Just thinking about my case."

Denise wrinkled her brow. "Hey, it's Friday night. No time to be thinking of work. Time to party. Jenny and I are going to the dance club outside of town. Want to join us?"

"Thanks, but I think I'll pass tonight. I might just walk around town a bit. Maybe go out by the water. I haven't been there yet."

"Well, you never know who you might run into." Denise gave her a wink. "See you later."

Colleen stayed at the bar long enough to finish her drink and then headed back to the Paper Nautilus. She wanted to get rid of her purse before she took her walk along the beach.

CHAPTER 8

The air had cooled considerably since sunset, and the wind coming off the ocean was almost chilly. Colleen walked along the water's edge and wished she'd worn more than the white sundress. The moon was full, shining a shimmering silvery path along water dark as velvet. The soft whoosh of the waves breaking along the sand was soothing and romantic. Colleen allowed the salt water to caress her ankles. She shivered at its first soft touch, but soon it felt warm. She headed south, toward the gay beach. To her right the brightly lit boardwalk was crowded with people. The noise from the amusement center carried across the sand. She could hear the sounds of the rides and games and the muted roar of voices and laughter. She was almost tempted to take a detour and play some pinball, but she continued her solitary walk.

Here and there she encountered others on the beach. Some men were night fishing, the moonlight glinting off their fishing lines like airplane beacons. A young couple lay in the sand, kissing and caressing each other. Colleen envied them their freedom to do so.

Soon the shops ended, and it was much more quiet. If she listened hard enough, she could hear crickets in the dune grasses lining the boardwalk. She still saw an occasional person walking on the board- walk, but the beach seemed empty. She felt totally alone and peaceful. She thought briefly about Smokey, and hoped that Brian was taking good care of him. She wondered if Gillian liked cats.

Colleen stopped and stared out over the ocean. The waves caressed her ankles, splashing little tentacles of water up her legs. Her thoughts drifted back to Gillian . . .

Gillian strode briskly along the boardwalk, dodging running children and groups of teenagers. The lights from the shops and arcades hurt her eyes, and the noise gave her a headache. She decided to walk on the beach instead and descended the first set of stairs she came to. She sat on the bottom step and took off her running shoes. Rather than carry them, she hid them under the boardwalk and hoped they'd be there when she came back.

The lone figure at the water's edge caught Gillian's eye. She stood slightly angled to the ocean so the moon caught her in its pale glow. The brilliant red-gold of her hair was muted in the soft light, the long curls blowing away from her face. Her white skin looked almost ghostly. The white sundress showed off wide shoulders and a bare back. Billowing behind her, her skirt was plastered tight against shapely legs. She carried sandals in her right hand. Colleen.

Gillian trembled. She couldn't remember feeling this way before. Protective. Cautious. Vulnerable.

Colleen seemed to take a deep breath and then turned toward the ocean. She began to take slow steps forward, kicking the water as it splashed her. The sight was so childlike, it made Gillian smile. She admired the sway of Colleen's hips as she negotiated the soft sand. Her feet sank into holes made by the water. A couple of times she held out her arms, as if to regain her balance. Colleen walked slowly down the beach. Gillian decided to follow, but at a distance.

Colleen let the image of Gillian drift from her mind. Her fantasy hadn't taken her beyond a kiss, but if she'd been alone in her bed, who knows what might have happened. It was getting late, and the romance of the evening was beginning to fade. The dark water looked menacing now. Her skin was gritty from the salt spray, and her eyes stung.

She walked away from the waves until she was on

dry sand. It felt so warm. She enjoyed the feel of it
between her toes. The dark form of the boardwalk
disappeared from her peripheral vision. She was at
Queen Street, the center of the gay beach. She was
surprised that she saw no one. Perhaps people were
being more cautious because of the recent gay
bashings. Suddenly she was nervous, aware that she
was alone at a deserted part of the beach. She felt
the skin on her neck prickling. She glanced toward
the boardwalk and saw a dark form emerge from the
shadows. She gasped and started to run toward the
water.

"Colleen!"

Colleen stopped and turned.

"I didn't mean to startle you," Gillian said as she
approached.

"How long have you been there? I didn't see
anyone."

"Well, I've kind of been following you."

"Following me? Whatever for?"

"You seemed so far away. I didn't want to disturb
you."

Colleen smiled. "I like being disturbed by you. I'm
happy that you're here." She touched Gillian lightly
on the forearm.

"Can I walk you back to town?"

"Of course. Shall we walk on the boardwalk or
down here?"

Gillian took Colleen's hand. "Let's stay by the
water. It's much more peaceful, don't you think?"

They walked in silence for a few moments.
Colleen looked at the profile of the tall woman beside
her. Gillian caught her staring and smiled. Colleen
felt unexpectedly shy, not knowing quite what to do.

It wasn't as if she had never been with a woman before, but this was different somehow.

"It's a beautiful night," she said. "I've never seen the full moon over the ocean before."

"Yes, no clouds tonight. What were you doing out here all alone?" Gillian's voice was almost a caress.

"Just didn't feel like spending the evening alone in my room. I wanted to start my weekend out right."

Gillian increased the pressure of her hand. "I think you will."

Her voice held hidden nuances that made Colleen blush. She lowered her head so her hair hid her face. This was what she had hoped for, and now she felt as shy as a junior high girl on her first date. She couldn't remember feeling this shy with Amy, or any other woman for that matter. She couldn't think of anything to say, but the silence was not uncomfortable.

She stopped walking so Gillian was forced to stop too. As Gillian looked at her in surprise, Colleen boldly put her hands around Gillian's head and pulled her face down. She ran her tongue lightly along Gillian's lips, savoring the slight saltiness. As their kiss deepened, she closed her eyes to the moonlit sky, hearing only the ocean as it brushed the shoreline. She was more bold, thrusting her tongue into Gillian's mouth. Gillian's mouth and tongue answered in kind, possessive and demanding. Her strong arms crushed Colleen to her chest. It was just like Colleen's fantasy, only this time it was real.

Gillian suddenly pulled away. The expression on her face told Colleen it wasn't what she really wanted to do. "I'm sorry, Colleen, but we need to be a bit more careful," she said, breathing heavily. She glanced up and down the beach, then relaxed. They were alone.

Colleen felt angry at the unfairness of it all. Gillian smiled at her reassuringly, as if reading her thoughts, then stopped and held up her index finger in a wait-a-second motion. She ran over to the boardwalk and returned with a pair of shoes. She took Colleen's hand once more, but at that moment some teenagers came running across the sand. Gillian let her hand slip from Colleen's.

"Let's keep walking," she said.

As they approached the more populated area of the beach, she motioned Colleen to follow her to the stairs. They sat together on the bottom step and put their shoes on. On the boardwalk once more, they stopped at one of the ubiquitous taffy and fudge shops. Colleen followed Gillian inside.

"You can't come to Rehoboth and not get fudge," Gillian informed her. "Look, every flavor you can imagine. What'll you have?"

"Anything with nuts," Colleen answered, pleased. Chocolate was her major vice. A woman who bought her chocolate was a woman after her own heart.

Gillian handed her a white box filled with at least a pound of the rich confection.

"How do you expect me to keep my girlish figure?" Colleen asked in as serious a tone as she could muster.

"Well," Gillian replied just as serious, "if you keep coming to my aerobics classes, I'll work it off of you."

"I'm sure you can think of a better way to work it off me," Colleen surprised herself in answering. It

102

was too late to back off now. She broke off a piece of fudge and put it slowly to her mouth. She got the response she wanted; Gillian's green eyes glittered with unspoken desire.

Colleen couldn't remember how they got to the Paper Nautilus. Her hands shook as she tried to unlock the door. She dropped the keys. Gillian picked them up and finished the task. In the darkness of her room, Colleen moved first. Holding both of Gillian's well-muscled arms, she raised her head for a kiss. Gillian's lips sent a bolt of electricity through her. Colleen trembled, and Gillian kissed her harder. Then Gillian slowly unzipped the sundress and pulled the thin straps over her shoulders. The dress slid down over her hips and landed in a heap around her ankles.

Gillian drew in a deep breath. Colleen wore only a pair of white satin panties. Her body was all womanly curves, softly rounded in all the right places. So different from the other women she'd been with, especially Candy. But none of that mattered now. She didn't want hardness and definition.

She pulled Colleen to her and kissed her neck, giving a little nip here and there. Colleen moaned and began to move seductively against her. Gillian could feel the desire stirring; her jeans suddenly felt too tight. Colleen grabbed hold of her shirt and pulled it off. The cool rush of air from the ceiling fan brushed gently across her breasts. Her nipples stood erect and Colleen placed her hot lips around one of them. Gillian leaned back against the wall, moaning as Colleen's sucking sent the sensations right between her legs. She continued sucking as she unbuttoned Gillian's jeans, then ran her hand over Gillian's crotch.

Who's in charge here, Gillian thought, and she pushed Colleen to the bed. Colleen made a little noise in her throat, as if disappointed that she no longer had Gillian's nipple in her possession. But she did not resist. Gillian liked that. Colleen lay on the bed, her legs draped over the side, her fiery hair tumbling and curling around her. Gillian lay beside her and ran her fingers along the swell of each breast. She enjoyed Colleen's in-drawn breath at her every move. She pulled her panties off, marveling. She'd never been with a redhead before.

When Gillian touched the tight red curls, Colleen pushed up against her hand. But Gillian pulled her hand away, wanting to savor the moment. She enticed Colleen slowly, sensuously, making each touch a hint of what was to come. She lay on top of her, holding Colleen's arms above her head as she kissed her. The scent of her perfume mingled with the scent of her passion. As Gillian moved her hips against Colleen's, she could feel the heat and wetness between her own legs.

Gillian brought her hand between Colleen's legs. Colleen gasped and opened wider as Gillian's fingers made their first tentative exploration. She was dripping wet, something Gillian expected yet was surprised by. Colleen moaned loudly as she thrust her hips forward, as if to take more of Gillian's hand into her. She inserted one finger, then another, then another. Colleen moved in rhythm with her thrusts. Gillian kissed her neck, her shoulders, her breasts, sucking in a rosy nipple. She withdrew her fingers and continued her path down Colleen's body, her tongue flicking over salty skin. Colleen grabbed her hair, pushing her downward.

Kneeling on the floor, Gillian parted that amazing red hair and let her tongue lick Colleen's clitoris ever so softly, letting Colleen's movement dictate the pace. And when Colleen's shuddering release vibrated beneath her, Gillian smiled in satisfaction. Smiled too with an emotion she hadn't felt before — and couldn't name.

Colleen woke early the next morning. She stretched, letting the sun from the open window caress her naked body. She was surprised to find herself alone in the bed. A note was propped up on the empty pillow.

Sweetie — Had to leave. You were beautiful.
See you in aerobics. G.

Colleen's body still tingled from their love-making the night before, and ached a little from the aerobics. The last time she remembered looking at the clock, it was four in the morning. It was only seven. How could she feel so energized after only three hours of sleep? She hugged her pillow and smiled, wishing she and Gillian could have stayed in bed all day. With a sigh, Colleen got up, showered, and dressed. Starving, she decided to forgo breakfast downstairs, going instead to the Dream Café.

When she got to the gym, she had almost an hour to wait for class to start. Gillian was not in yet. Colleen began her warm-up on the stationary bike. The memory of the previous night brought a smile to her lips and made her forget the aches and pains of yesterday's unaccustomed exercise.

Most of the patrons looked as if they had stepped right out of a fitness magazine. Except for one. He was a brute of a man, at least six-feet-five, with extraordinarily broad shoulders, a massive chest, and bulging arms. Strong, equally muscular legs could overtake a quarry with a few long strides. He looked like a caricature of a wise guy. His pock-marked face had never been handsome, with a permanent sneer and little black eyes like currants. The nose was surprisingly aquiline and looked out of place on the otherwise ugly face. The shoulder-length hair was the color of over-dried straw and looked to be just as dry and brittle. He was obviously into serious body-building, but he looked nothing like the men she'd seen in Brian's magazines. She had no idea how much weight was on the barbell that he lifted repeatedly to his chest, but it looked like an awful lot. Each lift was accompanied by a guttural growl. Suddenly, he looked straight at her. The hairs on her neck rose with fear, and she looked away quickly.

Someone tapped her on the shoulder and she let out a little scream of fright. Heart pounding, she looked over. It was Stephan. His expression of concern was almost comical.

"Didn't mean to scare you," he said. "You look like you've seen a ghost. Are you okay?"

She stopped pedaling and took a deep breath. "Yes. Sorry. Didn't mean to act like such a ninny." She lowered her voice. "Say listen, who is that guy over there?"

He followed her glance. His face took on a grim expression. "That's the lovely and talented Barry Charles."

"He frightens me."

"As well he should. I told you before to stay away from him. Now do you see why?"

"He looks like he walked right off of *America's Most Wanted*. Why didn't the police talk to him?"

Stephan gave a mirthless laugh. "You can't go after someone just because of how they look. Candy would never file a complaint against him. No one has ever formally accused him of selling drugs. Why should they suspect him any more than any other customer of the gym?"

"I still think you're crazy to let him come here. Surely he must frighten some of the other clients?"

Stephan shrugged. "If it makes you feel better, the community's aware of him. We know to be wary. As well you should."

"What does he do for a living?"

"Construction, odd jobs." Stephan grinned and gave her a wink. "Let's talk about something more pleasant. Gillian called to say she'd be a bit late this morning. You have anything to do with that?"

She blushed, but could say honestly, "I did not corrupt her."

"I'll have to take your word for it," he replied. "Don't worry, she'll be here for class. See you later."

"Wait, Stephan," she called out as he turned to go. "What have you decided to do about Phillip? Did you talk to him about coming home?"

The sadness in his dark eyes disappeared for a moment. "Yes. Yes. He wants to come home, like you said. He was afraid to ask. I'm leaving tomorrow, and if all goes well, we'll be back next Saturday."

She reached out and touched his arm lightly. "I'm happy for you both." He smiled and walked away. She resumed her pedaling.

Barry Charles was still growling. She shot surreptitious glances his way. He ignored her, absorbed as he was in his feats of strength. She noticed that no one else looked his way or worked out near him. It was as if he had the gym all to himself. He threw down the weight suddenly. Its crash startled a lot of people. He swaggered over to the rack of free weights and snatched up a towel, which he used to wipe his face. He looked around the room, catching sight of Colleen watching him once again. The look on his face was like that of a snarling dog. She felt the goosebumps rise on her skin, but she gave a small wave and tentative smile. She didn't want his anger directed at her. His expression relaxed and he disappeared into the men's locker room.

Colleen soon tired of the bicycle and decided to try her hand at free weights. She picked up the smallest dumbbells — five pounds each — and started doing bicep curls the way she had seen others do them. After about eight curls, her arms started hurting. She put the dumbbells down and eyed the barbell rack. The lightest one weighed twenty-five pounds. Surely she could curl twenty-five pounds. As she bent down to remove the bar from the rack, someone tapped her on the shoulder. She looked up into Gillian's smiling eyes.

"Well, hello there," Gillian said, her voice a caress. "Looks like you've been busy."

Colleen rose to her full height. "Have to be warmed up for your class."

"You were awfully warm this morning." Gillian's eyes moved slowly over her as she spoke. The message was unmistakable, and Colleen felt her cheeks redden. Gillian laughed softly. "Come on back. It's time for aerobics."

The room was full; at least twenty people were waiting. Gillian got up on the carpeted platform and turned on the music.

An hour later, Colleen again lay collapsed on her mat. It seemed as if every muscle in her body was rebelling. She closed her eyes and listened to the murmuring voices in the room. Then someone knelt beside her and kissed her lightly on the lips. She opened her eyes and smiled up at Gillian.

"You look beautiful," Gillian told her.

Colleen smiled and opened her eyes. "Why, thank you. You don't look so bad yourself. How did I do today?"

"I think you're pushing yourself too hard. But you did good." She ran her fingers suggestively over Colleen's bare arm. "Think you'll need a massage later for your aches and pains?"

"Mmmm. Sounds good to me."

Gillian grabbed Colleen's hand and pulled her to a sitting position and then up. "C'mon, I'm starved. Let's go for pizza."

Is this what it's like to fall in love, Colleen wondered as they strolled down the boardwalk. Nonsense, her sensible side said, you've only just met. She gazed at Gillian's strong profile and followed it down to the glittering gold chain encircling the long neck. Who had given her that piece of jewelry — Candy? An unknown lover she knew nothing about?

"You're awfully quiet," said Gillian, startling her.

"I . . . I was thinking about work," Colleen lied.

Gillian raised her eyebrows. "Work? On a beautiful day like this? It's the weekend, my dear. You'll have plenty of time to think about work soon enough. Besides, I've got plans."

My dear, Colleen thought, she called me *my dear.*

CHAPTER 9

Gillian's "plans" included trips to the quaint town of Milton to shop for antiques and to the Cape Henlopen nature reserve where they saw majestic great blue herons, graceful terns, delicate egrets, and even a gawky-looking pelican or two. It was a world that Colleen had only seen on National Geographic specials or read about in books. She felt like a child as she ran along the shore line, squealing in delight as she found a whelk or a seahorse or a pearlized shell abandoned by the retreating waves. Scrambling among the scrub pines that covered the sandy terrain, she discovered hermit crabs and strange-looking animal tracks. Suddenly, it was Tuesday, but Gillian enticed her away from work for one more day of fun and took her for a ride on the Cape May–Lewes ferry.

And the nights, oh, the nights. Colleen would bet that the Paper Nautilus hadn't seen or heard such passion before. Gillian brought her to heights she hadn't thought possible. In the mornings they would run into Suzanne or Vera or the other guests, who would all exchange knowing glances and secretive smiles. But Colleen didn't care. She couldn't remember being happier.

Then it was Wednesday morning. The alarm woke her at seven. She took a leisurely shower, her mind filled with memories of her days and nights with Gillian. She dressed casually in stone-washed jeans and a polo shirt in a shade of blue she'd been told brought out the blue of her eyes. Feeling guilty that she had slacked off work for two days, she was downstairs by eight. Alone on the porch, she poured a mug of coffee, and sat in the chair near the phone. She knew that Mr. Sampson always arrived early to the office. He picked up the phone on the third ring.

"Kevin Sampson here."

"Hello, Mr. Sampson," she said. "Colleen Fitzgerald."

"Colleen, Colleen. So, you done foolin' around on the beach yet?"

She didn't answer right away. Then she realized he thought he was making a joke. She gave a small laugh, which she knew he expected. "Not yet, sir. I still have quite a bit of work to do."

"Any progress at all?" She gave him a thorough

112

run-down of the case so far. "Sure sounds like Fidelity will have to pay out the bucks, eh? Big bucks too."

Based on what she knew, she had to agree with him, but she still wasn't 100 percent sure that Candy's death was an accident. And she wasn't ready to leave Gillian. She had to stall.

"Well," she answered, "I still want to check out a few more leads." There was silence on the other end of the line. "Just so we can show Fidelity that we covered all our bases on this one." She winced as the cliché left her lips, but she knew it was the kind of talk Sampson could relate to.

"You're a good kid, Fitzgerald, a good kid. Okay, you've got until the end of the week to wrap this thing up."

He hung up abruptly. She took a sip of coffee. It had a vanilla flavor this time. She was reading her notes when Denise swooped into the room, wearing the skimpiest of thong bikinis. Colleen wondered why she bothered wearing one at all.

"Hey, Colleen, you're up early." She grabbed a piece of cake and took a big bite. "Yum. Poppy seed."

"Well, I am here on business, after all."

Denise looked at Colleen over the top of her designer sunglasses. "You're not going to tell me that you've been *working* these last four days?"

"Everyone's entitled to a break," Colleen answered, trying not to sound annoyed.

"Hmmm. I can tell when it's time to change the subject. So, how's the investigation going?"

"Lots of speculation, and nothing concrete." Colleen sighed. "I can't figure out why the people who think Candy was murdered didn't make a big thing out of it — demand more of an investigation — that sort of thing."

"I guess they just want to get on with their own lives. That's what Jenny says all the time. Candy's death was a shock, but people move on."

"What do you know about Lori Kestler's boyfriend?"

"Albert Simmons? He's a jerk. Hates gays. We don't think he's involved with the bashings or the vandalism though. He's more of a behind-the-scenes kind of troublemaker. The kind who would send money to those hate groups."

"What about Candy and Lori? Was he jealous?"

Denise took a second slice of cake. "I only know what people told me. Candy's relationship with Lori took place about a year or so ago, most of it while Jenny and I were in school. You know how people talk. It was supposed to be a nasty breakup, and Albert was right there to pick up the pieces. Or maybe he's the one who broke up the relationship to begin with."

"Any idea why Candy didn't change her insurance policy after the breakup?"

Denise shrugged. "My opinion? I think she just never got around to it. Who thinks they're gonna die? She was young, healthy. Well, if you consider forty-one young. She probably figured she had plenty of time to make changes."

"Do you go to the gym at all? Have you met this Barry Charles fellow?"

Denise shuddered. "He's bad news. Candy thought he was dealing drugs."

"But do you *know* him? I need to talk to someone who really knows him."

"Actually, you might get some answers from Albert Simmons. He owns a gym in Ocean City, and I heard they had some kind of steroid problem there. Maybe Barry Charles is his supplier too."

Frustrated, Colleen didn't answer. She'd hoped to get answers out of Denise, rather than more gossip. She smiled at her. "Thanks for the info. Guess I'd better get back to work now."

Denise jumped up. "I wonder what's taking Jenny so long." She started toward the stairs and then turned. "How's Gillian?" she asked with a wink.

Colleen felt her cheeks grow warm. She nervously twirled a loose strand of hair. "Just fine, thanks."

"You know you'll be the envy of every single lesbian in town? And you moved so quickly too. How long have you known each other? Four, five days?"

"It's not like I had some grand plan."

Denise bounded up the stairs. "Teasing!" she called out.

Colleen finished her coffee and decided to visit Lori Kestler again. At this hour of the morning, the temperature outside would be bearable for walking the distance. She decided to forgo business attire and a briefcase. Lori might be less formal if she herself was dressed more casually.

Seeing it was going to be another perfect day, Colleen decided to walk to Lori's along the as yet uncrowded boardwalk. The ocean sparkled with splashes of sun, the white caps barely noticeable. She wondered if Gillian might enjoy taking a whale watch. The ferry ride had whetted Colleen's appetite for another boat trip. The thought of Gillian made her smile. Colleen knew Gillian would be getting ready for her aerobics class. She stopped suddenly. "I have no idea what Gillian does for a living," she said out loud. Surely she did more than teach a class one hour a day?

Before long, Colleen found herself standing in front of Lori's two-story house. Just as she started up the walk, Lori came through the door. She stopped short when she saw Colleen.

"What are you doing here?"

Colleen started toward her. "I was hoping we could talk again."

"I don't think we have any more to talk about. I didn't kill Candy. End of story."

Colleen gestured toward the door. "Could I please come in? Please?"

Lori seemed indecisive. Colleen wondered if Albert was home. Finally, Lori opened the door. "You can't stay long."

Once again, she led Colleen through the ornately decorated living room and into the sunny kitchen. This time Lori didn't ask if Colleen wanted something to drink. She opened her refrigerator and automatically took out a pitcher of iced tea. Silently, she poured the tea into a tall glass and handed it to Colleen, then poured one for herself. She sat at the kitchen table and motioned for Colleen to do the same.

"I know what people are saying about me. That I was just after Candy for her money and her celebrity status. Well, I *did* love her."

"The fact that you weren't together very long and

you left her for a man gives people the impression —"

"People don't know the whole story. They have no right to judge. Candy wasn't easy to live with, you know. I couldn't measure up to her standards." She gulped her tea, then slammed her glass down on the table. "And it was no picnic knowing every goddamn lesbian in town wanted her, and was just waiting for me to screw up so they could say 'I told you so.'" Lori stared at her defiantly.

Colleen tried her tea. It was tasteless. "I'm sorry to dredge up old history," she said softly, hoping to calm Lori down. After a few moments of silence, she tried a different tack. "You obviously cared a lot about Candy. Can you think of any reason why someone might want to kill her?"

Lori stood up and began to pace the room. "Look, even the police say it was an accident. It doesn't matter if a hundred people wanted to kill her, does it? Candy fucked up and she's dead. Why can't people just let it rest? Are gays that desperate for attention?"

Colleen frowned. She didn't like Lori's tone when she said the word *gays*. "Listen, do you know Barry Charles?"

Lori stopped pacing and began picking dead leaves off of a rhododendron. "I don't know him personally, but I know of him. Why?"

"I'm sure you know that Candy suspected him of selling steroids. I was wondering if your boyfriend — Albert is it? — has had trouble with him at his gym."

Lori wouldn't look at her. "I don't believe so."

"Are you positive? Someone told me otherwise."

Lori shot her an angry glance. "People should mind their own business. Albert is perfectly capable of taking care of himself and his gym."

"I'm not attacking Albert. I just thought he might be able to give me more information about Barry. If this guy had something to do with Candy's death, wouldn't you want him caught?"

Lori sat down and sighed. "Albert gets home early today. Why don't you come back around five. I'll tell him to expect you." She paused, then added, "Just don't mention that you came by to see me. I'll tell him you called to talk with him, okay?"

Colleen left her sitting pensively at the table and walked out through the ornate living room. As she passed a narrow table along the wall, a stack of canceled checks caught her eye. The name on the top one made her pause. SAMPSON. Glancing toward the kitchen, she snatched the check up. It was one of Lori's checks, made out to Kevin Sampson for $5000. She dropped the piece of paper as if it were on fire. What could this possibly mean? She debated whether to confront Lori with the check, then decided not to. There might be a legitimate reason for such a check. Perhaps a loan against the insurance policy? She'd call Lisa Anderson to find out.

Her next stop was the police station to speak with Officer Perry. Among other things, she wanted to verify Stephan's alibi. A bored-looking clerk in uniform looked up as she approached the counter.

Colleen smiled. "I'm looking for Officer Perry. Is he on duty?"

The clerk looked at his watch. "He's been on duty since seven this morning."

"Is it possible I could speak to him?"

"Well, he's out on the road somewhere. Can someone else help you?"

Colleen pulled out her ID. "I'd like to speak with the officer in charge of the Candy Emerson case."

The clerk lost his bored look and sat up. "What's this all about? That case is closed."

She peered at his name tag. "Officer Johnson?" He nodded. "The insurance company just wants to clear up a few things."

"Well, Andy's just left on a two-week vacation."

"Then perhaps you could answer some questions?"

"What is it you want to know?"

"Well, I'd like to verify Stephan Gray's alibi for one thing. I understand he was here at the station reporting a stolen vehicle at the estimated time of death."

The look on the clerk's face made it obvious that he could not help her, but he looked toward the ceiling as if thinking. "Can't say that I remember that."

She gave an exasperated sigh. "Could I please speak to someone who's in charge?"

"Just a minute," Officer Johnson said and disappeared into a back room.

Colleen had paced the stark lobby at least ten times before Officer Johnson returned with another man in tow. He was taller and a lot older. He did not look very happy. "Can I help you, Miss..."

Colleen held out her hand. "Fitzgerald. I represent

119

the D.C. firm of Sampson and Rhoades. I'm investigating the death of Candy Emerson. It's purely routine."

His hand was cold and moist. "Lieutenant Tucker. Why don't you come to my office?"

He led her down a dingy corridor painted a faded army green. The floor squeaked under the threadbare brown carpet. She followed him into his office and sat across from him in a straight-backed chair. He pushed some papers out of the way and put both elbows on the desk and stared at her. She waited for him to speak. When he did not, she took a deep breath and started over.

"As I said, I'm investigating the death of Candy Emerson. My files didn't include a copy of the autopsy report, and I was hoping I could get one from you."

"I suppose I can get you a copy. Nothing much to read though. She suffocated from the weight, pure and simple."

"I'd also like to verify Stephan Gray's alibi. Were you on duty the morning of Emerson's death?"

"Yes, I was. I signed the stolen vehicle report."

"Why wasn't that fact included in the police report?"

He gave her a look of exasperation. "I don't know how you do things in Washington D.C., Miss Fitzgerald, but here we don't waste time collecting alibis in accidental death cases."

"Point well taken, but you did consider the possibility of murder?"

He leaned back in his chair. "Of course we did, but there was no evidence to indicate this was anything other than an accident. Yes, we realize that she had two beneficiaries who stood to gain a lot of money, but as you said, the Gray fellow was here and so in the clear. The other one, Lori Kestler, is too small to have lifted those weights. And she and her boyfriend gave each other alibis."

"What if it were someone with a grudge? Or an anti-gay hate crime?"

"Look, it was an open and shut case. No sign of forced entry. Nothing missing. No witnesses. Inconclusive prints. Emerson's injuries were consistent with dropped-weight injuries. Why can't people just accept the facts? First the faggots in town wouldn't accept it, and now you."

She felt the hairs on her neck rise at his use of the derogatory term. She kept her voice neutral. "I'm not saying Fidelity doesn't accept her death as an accident. We just want to be absolutely sure that neither beneficiary could be responsible."

"You're wasting your time. And mine."

She shifted in her uncomfortable chair. The lieutenant began rocking back and forth in his. The squeak grated on her nerves. "So, in your opinion, there's no foul play, no possible gay bashing? What about the graffiti on the window?"

He gave a snort of disgust. "That's just teenagers having some fun. If those people wouldn't flaunt themselves, maybe they'd be left alone. Rehoboth used to be a nice family resort."

"So, you didn't investigate Candy's death as a possible gay bashing?"

He gave her a look of impatience. "I thought you were investigating the insurance angle. Are you from some state agency or something?"

Colleen stood up. She was getting nowhere.

121

"You've been very helpful," she said pleasantly. "If you'll give me a copy of the autopsy report, I'll be on my way."

He dismissed her by turning his back to her and pouring a mug of coffee from a pot on the credenza behind him. "Officer Johnson will get it for you."

Ten minutes later, autopsy report in hand, she left the station. It was no wonder that the gay bashings had gone unsolved. Rehoboth's police force seemed right out of a bad movie.

CHAPTER 10

It was mid-afternoon when Colleen entered Lambda Rising. Bianca was behind the register talking to a police officer who Colleen assumed was David Perry. As she came in, Bianca waved enthusiastically.

"Hey, Colleen! Just the girl I want to see," Bianca cried. "David and I were talking about you."

David was leaning against the counter, but stood as she approached. He was a Castro Street clone — stunningly gorgeous with electric blue eyes and sun-bleached curly hair. His chiseled face was an artist's dream — sculptured cheekbones, perfect white teeth, precisely trimmed mustache over full lips. Of medium height and build, he filled out the police uniform like a model. She knew he wasn't gay, but she was certain he drove the men crazy.

"Hi. I'm David, Bianca's cousin," he said, his voice a deep baritone. His handshake was firm.

"I was just at the police station looking for you," Colleen said.

He laughed. "I'll bet you had the pleasure of meeting Officer Johnson. Nice fellow, eh?"

She laughed too. "He must have gotten up on the wrong side of the planet this morning. I also met Lieutenant Tucker. He's a real gem too."

"Well, don't use him to measure the Rehoboth Beach police force. He's sort of on loan from Milton. Our regular lieutenant was injured in a car accident, and Tucker's filling in for the summer."

"Johnson filling in too?"

"Unfortunately, no. But the town's really trying to change attitudes. The force has had sensitivity training, not only as far as the gays go, but other minorities as well."

"Glad to hear it."

"So, did they give you what you need?"

"I got the autopsy report. The lieutenant said it was a pretty open and shut case."

He and Bianca exchanged a glance. "I know some in the gay community are not happy with that, but really, we have no evidence to suggest otherwise."

Colleen shrugged. "My boss figured as much. Guess I'll read over the police report again and then file my own. The insurance company will just have to pay up. I don't suppose it would do me any good to

124

wait around two weeks to talk to the investigating officer?"

David shook his head. "I think you'd be wasting your time. I know the guy, and he's pretty thorough. No anti-gay prejudices, if that's what you're thinking."

He leaned over the counter and gave Bianca a kiss on the cheek. "Gotta go, love." He turned to Colleen. "Nice meeting you. Maybe we could have dinner before you leave." He gave Bianca a wink and was gone.

Puzzled, Colleen turned to Bianca. "Did I just hear David ask me out on a date?"

Bianca laughed. "Not exactly a date, but I'm sure he was serious about dinner."

Bianca came around the counter and motioned for Colleen to follow her outside. Bianca lit up a cigarette. They settled into the chairs nearest the store. "So, what brings you by?"

"I wanted to ask you something."

Bianca said nothing. Colleen took a deep breath. "Where does Gillian work? Besides the gym, I mean."

"At home. She's a freelance writer now. Used to be a professional aerobics competitor. Traveled around a lot. Then she inherited her dad's fortune and didn't have to work anymore."

Colleen was startled. Gillian rich? "I had no idea," she said. This information certainly put a new light on things. "And where is home?"

"You spent the whole weekend with her and never asked her what she does or where she lives?"

A thoroughly embarrassed Colleen shook her head. "Just never got around to it. We stayed at Paper Nautilus."

"Well, Gillian hasn't been able to decide on a place yet, so she's rented a suite in one of the hotels. The big fancy one at the north end of the boardwalk. You've probably seen it."

"Yes, it's beautiful. So, she and Candy didn't live together?"

Bianca blew smoke rings before she answered. "Nope. I think she was waiting for Candy to make up her mind. You also have to remember that they kept their relationship very hush-hush."

"Do you think Gillian would mind if I called her? Some writers don't like to be disturbed."

Bianca smiled and gave her a wink. "She wouldn't mind if *you* called her. She was actually in here this morning wondering if I'd seen you. You two are just crossing opposite paths today." She scribbled the number on a scrap of paper and handed it to Colleen. "I expect she's ready for a break."

The Paper Nautilus was deserted. At least she'd have some privacy. Colleen's hand shook as she dialed Gillian's number. The husky voice on the other end gave her butterflies.

"Hello?"

Colleen took a deep breath. "Hi, Gillian. Colleen. I got your number from Bianca. Am I disturbing you?"

"Not at all. I was hoping you would call. Missed you in aerobics this morning."

Colleen felt a rush of blood to her cheeks as she heard the pleasure in Gillian's voice. "Do you think you could take time out for a visitor?"

"I'd love to. Why don't you come to my place and I'll order room service."

"Yes, Bianca told me you lived in a hotel. That must seem awfully impersonal at times."

"I actually like it. Someone comes in and cleans up after you. No towels to wash. No dishes either. Anyway, I'm in room seven ten. Beautiful view of the ocean. It's very romantic at night."

Colleen felt herself blush again. "I'll be there soon. Should I bring anything?"

"A bathing suit. We have a nice hot tub here."

"Okay. See you."

Colleen hung up the phone, then dialed the office, but Lisa had apparently left early. The idea of going alone to Gillian's hotel room made her nervous. She shook herself mentally. She was acting like a high school girl. She and Gillian had just spent a glorious four days together. What was there to be nervous about?

She looked at her watch. It was almost four. She remembered that she was supposed to go back to Lori's at five to talk to Albert. Damn. She'd have to postpone her visit with Gillian. She redialed Gillian's number and explained the situation.

"Why don't you come by afterward?" Gillian suggested. "You'll probably need the hot tub by then. Actually, would you like me to come?"

Colleen thought of a smart response, but decided there'd be plenty of time for erotic talk later. "Thanks, but no," she said. "I know that Lori's not your favorite person. I'll be by as soon as I can."

"See you later."

Colleen hung up and went to her room. She

found the new blue and white tie-dyed tanksuit she'd bought last night at Splash after Gillian had kissed her goodbye early in the afternoon. Previous commitment, Gillian had explained. Colleen had fought off the twinge of uncertainty and gone on a shopping spree. She threw the tanksuit and her Phantom of the Opera beach towel into her knapsack and hurried out the door.

In about forty minutes Colleen was back on Josephine Street, ringing the doorbell of the Grey Poupon house, as she'd come to call it. Expecting Lori, she was startled when a man answered. He was already scowling, his thick black eyebrows knotted tightly above his somewhat bulbous nose. He was tall and broad-shouldered with deeply tanned skin and acne scars on his face. His hair was shoe-polish black, his eyes like ripe olives.

"Can I help you?" he asked, but she suspected he already knew who she was.

"My name is Colleen Fitzgerald. I believe Ms. Kestler told you to expect me?"

He waved her inside with a hand that was huge, his fingers thick and puffy. They didn't seem to belong to him for he was in no way fat. Even with her limited exposure, Colleen could tell he was a bodybuilder. She walked to the kitchen for the second time that day, all the while feeling the hairs on her neck prickling as Albert silently followed her. She wondered if Lori was home. On the kitchen table stood the inevitable pitcher of pale iced tea.

"Drink?" Albert asked gruffly. He motioned toward the pitcher.

"I think I've had enough caffeine for the day," Colleen answered, though she was thirsty after her walk. "Perhaps some juice or water?"

He filled a glass with ice from the freezer and added water from the tap. She took it gratefully. "Thanks."

He sat at the table and stared at her. She chose to remain standing. She cleared her throat. "Mr. Simmons, did Ms. Kestler speak to you about my visit? Why I've come?"

"She said you want to know about steroid use at my gym. Well, there isn't any. I wouldn't allow that sort of thing."

He didn't meet her eyes, and she knew he was lying.

"I'm not here to accuse you of anything. I just wanted to know if you've ever had trouble with a man named Barry Charles."

"Can't say that I have, but I know who he is. He belongs to that dyke's gym, so why should he come all the way to mine?"

"Well," she continued, ignoring his remark, "Candy Emerson had trouble with him. He's a strong guy. Seems pretty mean. Mean enough to protect his money-making interests?"

"What does all this have to do with me and Lori? You're supposed to be some kind of insurance investigator. The police, the coroner, the papers — all say it was an accident. What's all this Cagney and Lacey bullshit?"

"There's no need to be hostile, Mr. Simmons. I'm just doing my job. You're sure Barry Charles never caused trouble at your place in Ocean City? If he's dealing here, I'm sure he'd try to hit all the gyms in the area."

Albert stood up angrily. "I'm not going to say it again. I've had no problems with him. Just tell your damn insurance company to pay up and stop wasting our time. Next time I talk to Kevin Sampson I'm gonna have a few choice words for him."

Colleen immediately thought of the check she'd seen earlier that day. "You've talked with Mr. Sampson? Why?"

Albert suddenly seemed nervous. "No, I've never talked to him. Maybe Lori has. You know, in connection with the insurance. I've things to do. You'll have to leave."

Colleen looked him square in the eye. "Mr. Simmons, the beneficiaries of an insurance policy would have no reason to talk to Mr. Sampson. We are an independent firm hired by insurance companies to investigate suspicious claims. Have you or Lori had personal contact with someone at my firm?"

He roughly moved the chair out of his way. "I told you. No. Now, I asked you to leave."

"Yes, you sure did," she said as she backed out of the kitchen. "I'll see myself out."

Colleen took a deep breath when she got outside. Her whole body was tense and her head ached. Gillian was right — she did need that hot tub now. As she strode down the walkway, she felt the hairs on her neck prickle again. Someone was watching her. She glanced back at the house. The curtain on a second-story window fluttered, but she couldn't see who stood behind it. She was glad to be leaving, and almost ran up Josephine Street.

It seemed like forever, but Colleen finally made it to Gillian's hotel — an imposing structure, fourteen stories high and occupying an entire block. Colleen wondered which of the balconies facing the ocean was Gillian's. She entered the opulent lobby and had to step back and stare. She felt as if she'd entered another time. The plush, overstuffed furniture was covered with gold brocade intricately embroidered with gold and silver threads. Giant potted plants rested on marble tables or in well-placed corners. Subdued lighting calmed the nerves and rested sun-weary eyes, and the deep, multihued Oriental carpet muffled all sound. The ivory-colored walls were covered with pictures and mirrors, all in gilt frames from a bygone era. Colleen turned in the direction of a twittering sound. An ornate gold cage housed tiny finches. She could only imagine what the cost of a room here must be, let alone a suite. She approached the front desk warily. The uniformed man behind it looked up immediately. A shock of reddish-blonde hair fell over his wide forehead. His round face was slightly red, as if he'd just had a chemical peel. Nondescript brown eyes peered at her from behind wire-framed glasses. A pale mustache barely covered his upper lip.

"May I help you," he said with a smile that showed all of his uneven teeth and his gums. She saw his eyes flick over her as if assessing whether she belonged there. She explained her business and, after a call to Gillian, he directed her to the elevators.

Colleen had the elevator to herself. After a quiet and smooth ride, it stopped at the seventh floor and the door opened with a soft whoosh. Colleen found herself staring at her reflection in a huge mirror that adorned the wall directly in front of the elevator. She looked windblown and frazzled. Her nose glowed pink; she'd gotten burnt on the long walk. She wished she'd stopped to shower and change before coming here.

The hallway was somber and quiet, the beige carpeting absorbing every footstep. She stopped before room 710 and hesitated as she raised her hand to knock. Perhaps she should go home first? Without warning, the door flew open and Gillian stood there. Her smile was warm and welcoming as she grabbed Colleen's hand and pulled her inside.

"I heard the elevator ring and hoped it was you." She shut the door and hugged Colleen close. "I am so glad you're finally here." She kissed Colleen deeply.

"Me too," Colleen said when the kiss ended. She could already feel the warmth coursing through her body. She looked down and then at Gillian again. "You'll have to forgive my appearance. I just walked from Lori's house."

Gillian led her into the living room. "You look great. Wild and untamed. I like that."

Colleen glanced around the big room. Stark white walls and carpeting were accented by pink and lavender. Bright light came through the large balcony door and added to the light from strategically placed halogen lamps. The soft sounds of Cris Williamson came from a CD player situated next to a huge television. Colleen was surprised to hear it. Everyone she knew played Melissa Etheridge or Ani Difranco or the Indigo Girls.

The room was so perfect, so sterile, she was afraid to sit down. She put her knapsack gently on the floor next to the pink and lavender couch and stood with her hands in her jeans pockets.

"So, you like Cris Williamson? Don't hear her much anymore."

"Yeah, Suzanne and Vera were playing her one day. Women's music they called it. I heard it and got hooked. Bianca special-ordered the CD for me. It's nice background music when I'm writing."

"An older lesbian I know introduced me to Cris' music too." Colleen smiled. "So, how was your day?"

Gillian plopped onto the couch. "Productive. I finished an article for *Aerobic World Magazine*." She patted the seat next to her. "Relax, Colleen. I won't bite."

"Look, I feel really hot and sweaty. Would you mind terribly if I took a shower? That's tacky, I know."

Gillian jumped up. "Don't mind at all. Right this way."

She led Colleen down a long hallway. They passed a small kitchen on the right and a bedroom on the left. A bathroom came up on the right, but Gillian led her past that and into the master bedroom. White was again the dominant color, accented with pale mauve. The king-size bed, covered with a cherry-red quilt, dominated the room. Colleen knew the quilt could not be a hotel staple.

As if reading her thoughts, Gillian said, "I bought that quilt at an Amish market in Lancaster. Isn't the color marvelous?"

Four stairs led down to the master bath. It was a big room, and all the fixtures were furnished with the latest in bathroom gadgetry. The decor was all white and black and gold. The Jacuzzi was big enough for four people. Next to it, big fluffy towels with the hotel's crest, in gold of course, rested on a white wicker stand.

"This is quite a hotel suite," was all Colleen could think of to say. She felt foolish standing in the midst of all this luxury.

Gillian laughed. "Not what you expected, eh? It's comfortable, even if it is a bit ostentatious. I'm sure you much prefer the Paper Nautilus."

"Yes, I do." Colleen eyed the room. "It's impressive, but I don't much like it."

Gillian shrugged. "My father's lawyer actually made these arrangements for me. When I got here, I just didn't feel like finding another place. Besides, it's close to the gym."

After Gillian left, it took Colleen a few minutes to figure out how to turn the shower on. Her first attempt got her sprayed in the face with ice-cold water. She stifled a little shriek and adjusted the knob. She stripped quickly and stepped under the warm water. She stood still a few moments, letting it flow over her, taking the grime off her body and washing her tension down the drain. Lathering up with Gillian's soap gave her a secret thrill. It had a pleasant scent, like sandalwood. Her shampoo was of the common drugstore variety and smelled like almonds.

Feeling completely refreshed, Colleen stepped from the tub and grabbed a big, fluffy towel. It was as soft as it looked. She dried quickly and realized that she'd not brought a change of clothes. All she had in her knapsack was a bathing suit, and that was out in the living room. On the bathroom door, however, hung a white terrycloth robe. She hoped Gillian wouldn't mind her borrowing it. With a deep breath, she walked barefoot to the living room.

CHAPTER 11

Gillian heard the whisper of footsteps on the plush carpet. She looked up from the CD player and took a deep breath. Colleen stood before her, her skin still moist and pink from the shower. Her red hair fell straight and darkly wet to her shoulders, but already the ends were beginning to curl. Her blue eyes sparkled like sapphires in the sun. Gillian knew Colleen was naked underneath the white robe, and the thought sent shivers of anticipation up her spine.

"Feel better?" she managed to ask in a calm voice, forcing her attention to the task at hand.

"What would you like to hear now? Jazz? Rock and roll?"

"I'm not particular."

Colleen sat on the couch and crossed her legs. Gillian saw a flash of smooth thigh. She decided to go for background mood music and found Máire Brennan.

"I have some champagne chilling," Gillian offered. "Would you like a glass? I have strawberries too, just like in that movie. What was it?"

"*Pretty Woman,* but I'm like Edward in the movie. I don't drink alcohol. Sorry. I love strawberries though."

Gillian was slightly surprised at Colleen's revelation that she didn't drink. She didn't really like champagne all that much herself, but it seemed the romantic thing to do. "I have soda too, or iced tea."

Colleen grimaced. "Please, no iced tea. I've had enough bad tea to last a lifetime."

"Oh?" Gillian said as she went into the kitchen and opened the refrigerator.

Colleen followed and stood in the doorway. "Lori Kestler makes the worst tea I've ever tasted. Do you have Seven-Up and lime?"

Gillian straightened up. "No, but I'll get room service to bring some. How about some food too?"

"Sounds great."

They walked back into the living room. When Colleen sat back on the couch, the robe fell away from her leg. She did not move to close it. Gillian was beginning to feel very warm. She was getting that familiar ache between her legs. She realized that Colleen was teasing her, and doing a very good job of it too.

"I think I'll take a quick shower too," Gillian said with a smile. "You make yourself comfortable. Shall I see if I have something you can wear?"

This time Colleen pulled the robe around her legs. "Please."

Gillian groaned inwardly. When Colleen said please in that tone, she wanted to push her back into the couch cushions and make her beg for mercy. She sucked in a deep breath and went to her bedroom. She glanced over her shoulder. Was it her imagination, or was Colleen hiding a smile behind her hand?

In the bedroom, Gillian made the call to room service and undressed. Her shower was quick and hot. She was naked and vigorously rubbing her head with a thick towel when she sensed Colleen's presence in the doorway. Her image appeared through the swirling clouds of steam. She caught her breath as Colleen let the white robe fall from her body, giving Gillian a feeling of déjà vu.

"When is room service coming?" Colleen asked softly. The sensuous sway of her hips made it obvious she hoped not for a long while.

Gillian didn't answer, instead grabbing her tightly and kissing her with uncontrolled passion. Colleen's response was submissive yet no less demanding. She took Gillian's hands and placed them on her breasts. Gillian squeezed them softly, flicking gently at the nipples. She felt the moan deep in Colleen's throat as she moved her lips over Colleen's neck and shoulders. She ran her hands down Colleen's sides, letting them flow over rounded hips and to the back to cup soft buttocks.

Still kissing Colleen deeply, Gillian brought her

slowly to the plush white carpet. Colleen's hair fanned out beneath her, and she pushed herself against Gillian, the urgency of her passion driving Gillian into a frenzy.

"Patience, my sweet," she crooned into Colleen's ear, forcing herself to go slow.

"Take me, Gillian," Colleen answered. "Take me."

She almost obeyed Colleen's plea, but instead ran her hands slowly down Colleen's sides, letting them rest on curvaceous hips for a moment before moving up again. She kissed Colleen's neck, then moved her lips and tongue down across her sensitive collarbone and into the valley between her breasts. She moved her hands upward again as her mouth moved downward. Colleen's body writhed beneath her, her moans soft, almost whimpers. Gillian progressed lower still. Colleen's movement took on a greater urgency. Gillian laughed softly. She loved this woman's response to her. She breathed in the scent of sandalwood, mingled with the womanly scent of passion. She flicked her tongue gently, but Colleen grabbed her head and pushed her inward. She let her tongue probe deeply. Colleen's moans grew louder.

Gillian resisted the urge to bring Colleen to climax, instead teasing her with little licks and bites and sucks. She kissed her in the soft moist folds between her legs. She caressed Colleen's breasts, squeezing gently and catching rosy nipples between thumb and forefinger. Finally, when she herself could wait no more, Gillian stopped her teasing and gave Colleen what she wanted.

She felt Colleen's legs tighten. Colleen grabbed Gillian's hair and drew in a deep breath. For a moment there was silence, then Colleen let out a long drawn out sigh as she arched her back. Gillian felt the tension in Colleen's legs release. She lay limp as Gillian continued to kiss her softly.

"Come here," Colleen said moments later as she yanked gently on Gillian's hair. "I want you."

Colleen's hands started their own exploration of Gillian's curves. In the haze of her own desire, Gillian heard a sound. She ignored it, until it became an insistent banging. She sat up suddenly.

"Oh, my God, room service!"

"So soon?"

Gillian gave Colleen a quick kiss on the cheek and stood up. She could feel the wetness flow between her own legs as she pulled on the white terry robe Colleen had worn earlier. "Sorry, my love."

Colleen walked slowly down the hall. She had gone into the bedroom and found another robe in Gillian's closet. This one was purple silk, and somehow she knew it didn't belong to Gillian. She wore nothing underneath. She couldn't believe she had been stupid enough not to bring a change of clothes. Still, there was something very erotic about wearing nothing but a silk robe.

She didn't see Gillian at first, but the clatter of stainless steel against porcelain drew her attention to the open glass door. Their meal was set up on the balcony. On the table was a centerpiece of yellow irises and tiny white mums.

"There you are," Gillian said. If she was startled to see Colleen in the silk robe, she gave no sign.

140

"It's beautiful out here." A nice breeze was coming off the ocean.

Gillian took the covers off both plates. "I think the chef has outdone himself tonight. It's as if he knew this was a special occasion."

"Is it?" Colleen asked flirtatiously.

"Having my favorite girl to my room? You bet it's special."

The dark rippling water met a horizon that glowed pink and blue and lavender and yellow. The sound of the waves against the shore mingled with the cries of sea gulls and the murmur of voices on the boardwalk below. Colleen felt content.

"I love the view here," Gillian said, breaking the silence. "I think that's one reason why I stay."

"Surely you could find a house on the beach?"

Gillian bit into her fish. "Yes," she said between mouthfuls. "I imagine I will someday, but I haven't decided if I'm going to live in Rehoboth permanently."

Colleen tried the fish. It was succulent and baked to perfection. "I think I could live on the beach all year. The problem would be finding a job. I guess I could commute to Ocean City or Salisbury."

"Tell me about yourself. Your family. Do you like your job? The city?"

"Well, my parents live in a D.C. suburb. Mom stays home and dad works as an electrician. My brother, William, also lives nearby. He's married and has three children, with a fourth on the way. Good Irish Catholic family. My sister, Meagan, lives in Portland. She had one daughter and then had her tubes tied. Mother would be shocked if she knew. She doesn't believe in birth control. Always regretted that she only had three children. Wanted to be like Robert and Ethel Kennedy."

"You're the youngest?"

"Yes, but we're very close in age. Meagan is thirty-four and William just turned thirty."

Gillian looked surprised. "How old are you?"

"Twenty-seven."

"For some reason I thought you were younger."

Colleen smiled. "Well, how old are you?"

"Thirty-two. So, tell me about your job?"

"I've worked for Sampson and Rhoades Investigations for only six months. Before that I was a nine-one-one dispatcher for five years, believe it or not. I had a liberal arts degree and went back to school for a major in Police Science. Toyed with the idea of law school, but decided it was too much work. Anyway, insurance companies hire us to check into claims they find suspicious. I'm very surprised that Mr. Sampson — he's the head honcho — sent me out alone on this assignment. I'm still kind of a trainee."

"Why do you think he did it?"

Colleen put her fork down. "That's what I wanted to talk to you about. You see, when I visited Lori Kestler earlier today, I saw a check for five grand made out to Kevin Sampson. Later, Simmons indicated that he'd talked to Mr. Sampson, but in the next sentence denied it and said Lori must have spoken to him. I have a strong feeling that those two are involved in Candy's death."

"I wish I could help you, Colleen, but I don't know anything. Really. None of us want to believe that Candy was careless, but she was known to work out alone. Accidents do happen, even bizarre ones."

142

"Well, I've ruled out Stephan, and I know Lori couldn't have done it alone. She threw me some fish story about a transsexual bodybuilder who was afraid Candy would expose her. Some sort of major rival during her competition days."

Gillian's hearty laughter rang out. "You must be talking about Robbie Taylor. She may look pretty masculine, but she's no transsexual. You see, contestants at pro events like Ms. Olympic Universe are required to submit their birth certificates to prove they're female. The promoters want no hint of scandal. No, if she had some dark secret, it certainly wasn't that."

"But could there be something? Lori told me that Robbie dropped out of a competition suddenly. A competition Candy subsequently won." Colleen persisted.

"I really think that's a dead end. Competitors drop out at the last minute for all kinds of reasons. Illness. Family problems. I've done it myself. What else do you have?"

"Barry Charles, the alleged steroid dealer. He's certainly capable. Very strong. A homophobe from what I've heard."

Gillian was somber. "He did give Candy a hard time. She talked to me only a little about it. Felt she couldn't go to the police unless she had proof."

"What about just a random killer? I know there's been trouble in town with assaults on gay men. Someone sees an opportunity to get rid of a lesbian and takes it."

"But the doors were locked from the inside. If someone killed her, they had to have been in the gym all night. And how would they hide from Stephan? He closes up."

"He could've been distracted that night. Some bad news about Phillip?"

Gillian got up and put her arms around Colleen, kissing her lightly on the neck. "It's a beautiful night," she said. "I think we have some unfinished business. Do you really want to talk about death and hatred?"

Colleen sighed. She took Gillian's hands in her own. The sunset was complete, and she looked out over the dark, quiet beach. The sky was a deep velvet blue, littered with thousands of glittering stars. How could murder happen in this peaceful little town? She stayed quiet and still. She felt as if she belonged here. Here in this hotel suite with Gillian, in this town, in this community. It was amazing how a few days could change your life. It would be hard to return to D.C., to her lonely little apartment that she had loved so much, to her new job.

"You're right," she said. "How about that trip to the hot tub? I bought a new suit for the occasion."

"Mmmm. Is it a bikini?"

Colleen laughed. "No way. Got to take a few more aerobic classes before I try one of those."

Gillian stood up. "Okay, let's go." She pulled Colleen out of the chair, and Colleen had the feeling that their trip to the hot tub would be very brief.

CHAPTER 12

The next day, after aerobics and a quick bite at the Dream Café, Colleen returned to the Paper Nautilus to make some calls.

She reached Brian at Lambda Rising in Washington. The bookstore was too crowded for a real conversation. He only had time to report that the "hideous little fur ball" threw up on his best pumps and his lawyer would be contacting her. Still laughing, she dialed the office. Lisa answered immediately.

"Hi, Lisa. It's Colleen. I need you to do me a favor."

"Sure thing," Lisa answered. "Enjoying your stay at the beach? You've had perfect weather for it."

"That's for sure. I hate to think of coming home."

Lisa's voice dropped to a whisper. "Met any cute guys? I'd go crazy seeing those half-naked bodies on the beach."

"Sure, there's lots of cute guys," Colleen said, thinking of Stephan and Officer Perry, "but I'm here to work."

"Oh, please! Now, what do you need?"

"I need you to check the Candy Emerson account and see if any loans were drawn against the policy. By Lori Kestler in particular."

"Hold on a minute." Colleen could hear the sounds of computer keys being tapped. "No, nothing here. Why?"

Colleen wondered just how much she should reveal, but decided she had to trust Lisa. "I saw a check made out to Mr. Sampson from Lori. It was for five thousand dollars. Lisa, why would she be paying him such a large amount, and for what?"

"Hold on a minute." Colleen heard her put the phone down, then the sound of her footsteps. She heard a door slam. Lisa picked up the phone again and spoke, her voice low. "This is really weird. Do you think he could be involved in some big cover-up?"

"Oh, Lisa, no need to be so melodramatic. I'm sure there's a perfectly reasonable explanation. Maybe by some strange coincidence he knows Lori personally." She paused. "But why wouldn't he have told me?"

"Well, I hate to bring this up, but don't you think it's a bit odd that he sent you to investigate this case? I mean, you've only been here for six months, and you've never been given an assignment. I would think the least he'd do is send someone with you."

"I guess I was so excited to be going, I didn't think about it. He said he wanted to see how 'tough' I was. Hey, when you've been pushing papers for so long, you're glad for a change. But listen, I'm going to fax you my notes so far. Could you do background checks on the people for me?"

"No problem. Also, let me see if I can do some discrete nosing around. Sampson's secretary likes me. I'll call you tonight when I get home."

"I'm going to dinner at seven, so it needs to be before that or else tomorrow." She and Gillian had agreed to meet at Mano's.

"Mmmm. Dinner? Lucky girl. Hope he's cute."

"Yeah," Colleen answered vaguely and hung up before Lisa could ask any pointed questions.

At that moment, Jenny and Denise bounded into the house. "Hey!" Denise called out. "Where ya been? We looked for you last night at Square One."

"I just had a lot of work to do."

"We're going to Lewes this afternoon to take a dolphin cruise. Want to come along?"

It certainly sounded like more fun than visiting Barry Charles, but she had to say no. The energetic duo shrugged in unison and disappeared up the stairs. Back in her room, Colleen retrieved the police file. She wondered if she should show it to Gillian, who would perhaps see it with a fresh eye.

The autopsy report was brief and to the point.

Death by strangulation, brought on by a heavy weight to the throat and chest. The crush injuries and bruises to the chest muscles were consistent with such an accident. Fingernails torn and bloody, but the coroner assumed it was from clawing at the barbell. He didn't find it necessary to take scrapings. That seemed odd to Colleen. Thinking about it, though, she concluded it was consistent with the theory that the police didn't do a thorough job. Candy had four small insect bites on one arm. No signs of an allergic reaction or anaphylactic shock. No history of epilepsy or other brain disorders. Death occurred sometime between four and six in the morning. Colleen knew Stephan had gotten to the gym around six-thirty, and Candy was already dead.

She examined the photos of the scene. The first time she'd looked at them, she'd almost gotten sick. No amount of news broadcasts or slasher flicks could prepare you for actual police photos of a crime scene, or potential crime scene. Colleen knew nothing of bodybuilding, but the barbell that crushed Candy's chest looked to be inordinately heavy. The different-sized weight plates were placed in random order on the barbell. Towels, dumbbells, and other plates were strewn on the floor near the bench. Candy's pretty face was distorted into a gruesome semblance of the one in the competition photos that adorned the walls of the gym.

Colleen threw the papers onto the bed. There was really nothing here for Gillian to see, or anyone else to see for that matter. She should just wrap things up, tell Mr. Sampson that Fidelity had to pay, and go on home. But that check from Lori really bothered her. And Albert's hostility was too intense. Something just didn't sit right with her.

Colleen left the papers on the bed and took a short trip across the street. She found Bianca sitting outside the bookstore, the inevitable cigarette in one hand and a novel in the other. Bianca's bright blue eyes lit up when she spied Colleen.

"Hey, girl. How's the case coming?"

Colleen sat next to her. "To tell you the truth, I think I'm just about done. I can't find any proof that it wasn't an accident, or any evidence to tie Stephan or Lori to Candy's death, which is what I was sent to do. If someone did murder her, it wasn't either of them."

"I could have told you that."

"Yes, you and everyone else. I'm going to try to talk to Barry Charles one more time, but I think it will be futile. Besides, if he did it, that doesn't affect the insurance claim."

Bianca took a deep drag of her cigarette. "Well, I for one feel better just knowing you did a thorough investigation. That's what the community wanted. It's what Candy deserved." After a moment of silence, she continued, "So, to change the subject. How's things with Gillian?"

Colleen didn't blush this time at the mention of her name. "Good. We get along really well. She's a wonderful person."

Bianca laughed. "Oh, come on now. You sound like you're describing a new roommate or a new sister-in-law."

This time Colleen did blush. "Okay. It's fantastic. I think I'm falling in love, if that's possible so soon.

Meeting Gillian is the best thing that's ever happened to me."

"You ever had a long-term relationship before?"

"Well, my most recent one lasted three years. I've been single a little over a year. Dated three or four women, but no one really caught my interest."

"It's easy to be smitten by Gillian," Bianca said between smoke rings. "Half the lesbians in town would give their right breasts to be with her. You must be really special."

"Bianca, you're embarrassing me."

"Sorry, dear. Just telling the truth." She glanced at her watch and stood up. "The lunch crowd should be coming by any time now." As if on cue, several men and women came walking up the sidewalk.

Colleen reluctantly went on her way. This meeting with Barry Charles was not something she really wanted to do, and it was true that if Barry was the murderer, it had nothing to do with her case. Still, she felt like it was a loose end that needed to be tied up.

Soon she found herself standing in front of the house on Felton Street. It looked as eerie as she remembered, the skeletal tree still standing guard. She squared her shoulders and strode up the short pitted walkway to the front door. She paused on the stoop and took a deep breath. Before she could knock, the door flew open. Barry Charles stood before her, barefoot and shirtless, wearing only a pair of ragged cut-offs. His over-developed build bulged with muscles that Colleen couldn't even imagine. She remembered well the scarred face and brittle yellow hair. He held a can of Red Wolf lager.

"Want something?" he snarled.

She pulled her ID from her back pocket and handed it to him. He gave it a cursory glance and practically threw it back at her. "Could we talk just for a few minutes?" she asked.

He took a noisy gulp of beer before crushing the can in his hand and throwing it into a holly bush. He stayed planted in the doorway and glared at her. "Nothin' to talk about."

"I'm looking into Candy Emerson's death," she went on as if he hadn't spoken. "I understand you're a member of her gym?"

"So?"

"Do you know if she had any enemies? Trouble at the gym? Problems of any kind?"

"That little faggot send you? You tell him he'd better stop making accusations or I'll sue his sorry little ass."

She took a deep breath. It was a mistake to have come. She now had to end the interview amicably. "If you're talking about Mr. Gray, he did not send me and has not accused you of anything. I'm here on insurance business, nothing more."

He pulled a crumpled cigarette from his back pocket and straightened it out slowly before putting it to his mouth. She watched him light it. His big, beefy hands made her shudder. He expelled a long puff of smoke in her direction.

"Look," he growled, "I know that goddamn dyke was trying to lay some drug-dealing rap on me, and now that fairy partner of hers is taking over where she left off. I wasn't involved in her death, though I'm not sorry it happened. These damn queers come to town and take over all the businesses. Don't know why Mark had to sell the only gym in town to a couple of queers. Would have bought the place myself if I'd had the money."

Colleen gritted her teeth. "As I said, Mr. Gray has nothing to do with this."

He gave a snort of derision and deliberately threw his lit cigarette butt in her direction. She refused to flinch. "You queer-lovers make me sick. Hell, you could be a dyke too for all I know. Now, get off my property. I have nothing else to say to you."

She turned on her heel without a word and marched off. She was seething inside.

He called out after her, "And you can tell Mr. Pretty-Boy Gray that he'll quit the gym before I do."

Colleen felt sick to her stomach. The hate emanating from the man was almost palpable. She could feel the sweat break out on her body. A dry, clammy sweat. The sweat of fear.

As soon as she knew she was out of view of the house, she sat on the curb and sobbed. Great heaving sobs that tore from her throat. She wanted to scream, to pound her fists into a wall or a tree. Something to release the tension and frustration. Instead, she clasped her hands around her arms and rocked back and forth, letting the tears fall and wash the numbness from her brain. She felt almost violated.

When the tears finally stopped, she took a deep breath and rested her arms on her knees to cradle her head. She could feel the heat of the sun against the back of her head. Its warmth spread through her body, comforting her. She didn't know how long she sat there on the curb, but someone touched her gently on the shoulder.

"Are you feeling okay?" a whispery voice asked.

Colleen looked up into the face of an elderly woman whose pale gray eyes were full of concern. Her white halo of hair was almost transparent, and she had more wrinkles than Colleen had ever seen on one person. Her stooped shoulders were covered with a ivory-colored shawl and she carried a cane.

Colleen smiled. "Yes. I just had to rest a bit. I'm not used to this heat."

The woman pointed an arthritic finger. "I live in that house there and I saw you come. You've been sitting here about thirty minutes. I was concerned."

Colleen stood. The woman barely reached her chest. "Thank you, but I'm okay now." She held out her hand.

The woman placed a shaking hand into hers. The skin felt as soft as tissue paper, and as fragile. Colleen gave a gentle squeeze and smiled once more before she let go.

"You be careful in this heat," the gentle voice admonished her, "and wear a hat."

CHAPTER 13

The loud banging penetrated Colleen's consciousness. "Colleen!" Suzanne's voice called out. "Your
phone call. Colleen, can you hear me?"

"Yes. Yes," Colleen answered. "I'll be right down."

She sat up groggily and shook her head. How
long had she been napping? She fumbled for her
clock. 6:00. She'd been sleeping nearly three hours,
and she had to meet Gillian at seven. She jumped
out of bed and threw on her robe before racing down
the stairs. Suzanne was nowhere in sight. Colleen
snatched up the phone.

"Lisa?"

"Where the hell have you been? I was just about to hang up."

"Sorry, I was sleeping. Not feeling too well. Do you have something for me?"

"I haven't had a chance to ask Mr. Sampson's secretary any questions, but I have a report for you on your list of suspects. I hope you realize I'm calling after hours."

"Yes, of course. I appreciate it. Now, what do you have?"

Colleen heard papers being shuffled. "Let's see," Lisa said, "the first one on the list was Stephan Gray. Nothing as far as a criminal record goes, a few traffic tickets here and there. Lots of debt though. Mortgaged to the hilt, even his share of the business. Most of the funds going to some clinic in Mexico. Owes money to a hospital here in the States too. He even cashed out his own life insurance policy."

"Okay, I knew that. What else?"

"Barry Charles. Now, there's a guy who's real trouble. We've got a couple of assault arrests. Charges dropped 'cause the victims recanted their accusations. Trouble with drugs in New York, but not enough evidence to convict. Assaulted a police officer after being stopped for a traffic violation. Served two years for that, then paroled for good behavior. Got into a fight at some bar and tore the place up. Had to pay damages, but no jail time."

"Did the report say what the drugs were?"

"Now that's a funny one to me. Steroids. Says here he used to hang out at high school athletic meets. Football games, wrestling matches, track and field."

"Candy Emerson was allegedly having trouble with him for the very same thing. I've spoken with him. He really hated her."

"Do you think he could have killed her?"

"Certainly was strong enough."

Lisa shuffled more papers. "Okay, Lori Kestler. Pretty clean. Her money is tied up with some gym in Ocean City." There was more crackling of paper. "The Iron Workout. Hmmm. Seems it's on the verge of bankruptcy. Her share of the insurance will help there."

"That's probably the boyfriend's gym. Anything else?"

"Got into an altercation at some bodybuilding event. Threw a shoe at one of the competitors on stage. Escorted out and told never to come back."

Colleen stifled a laugh. "Does it say who the object of her ire was?"

"Someone named Robbie Taylor. She wouldn't press charges though. What is it with these people? No one ever wants to press charges."

"Guess assault with a shoe doesn't rate. How about Albert Simmons?"

"He's got a rap sheet too. Oh yes, The Iron Workout does belong to him. Seems he lives high on the hog and that is why he's ready to declare bankruptcy. Expensive house in Rehoboth, high-priced cars, including a classic Jaguar."

"Wait a minute. I was told the house belonged to Lori."

"Let's see, she owns a house on Josephine Street. Also mortgaged to the hilt. His is a rental property on the beach. Charges three grand a month. Must be a palace at that rate. Anyway, he's had some racial discrimination charges brought against him in relation to the gym. One by a prospective employee and two by prospective clients. The employee settled out of court — another reason for Albert's money troubles — and the other two are pending. Nice bunch of people you've got there."

"Well, they've all got a motive for wanting Candy dead, and it's the same one. Money. Trouble is, can't link any of them to opportunity. The gym was locked. What else?"

"Hmmm, this Robbie Taylor person is clean too. Lives in Philadelphia now. She had a libel suit against some tabloid for claiming she was a transsexual." Lisa laughed.

"Nothing to tie her in to Candy?"

"Not unless she could lift a barbell while sitting in a wheelchair."

"Wheelchair?"

"Yeah, seems poor Robbie was in a car accident about fourteen months ago. Almost died. She's a paraplegic now."

"Oh, that's awful. I was considering taking a trip to see her, but guess I don't need to now."

"Some way to end a bodybuilding career, eh? Let's see. You've got two college kids on the list too, but they're inconsequential."

"Could you go ahead and fax me this stuff? I've got to get ready for dinner."

"Wait a minute," Lisa interrupted, "don't you want to hear about Gillian Smith?"

Colleen was taken aback. "Gillian?"

"Yeah, you have her down as Candy's ex-lover, remember?"

Colleen hesitated. Did she really want to hear this? "Well, okay. Yeah. Tell me what you have."

"Nothing much, except that she was on five years' probation for forging checks. Other than that, clean record. No recent money troubles. She inherited a fortune last year from her father. He made his money on Wall Street. And..." Lisa paused for effect. "...he died of insulin poisoning. Ruled an accidental death. Sounds a little Klaus von Bulow to me, eh?"

"Forged checks?" Colleen squeaked.

"Yeah. Funny thing is, it was her own father who brought charges. Guess that's why she got probation instead of prison."

Colleen just wanted to get off the phone. "Thanks for all your help, Lisa. I owe you a dinner."

"Two dinners."

Colleen hung up the phone slowly. Gillian forging checks? Having a criminal record? And her father's "accidental death." A horrible thought crossed her mind. Could Gillian have been involved in Candy's death? What if Gillian was only romancing her to distract her from the case? It was time to ask Gillian some questions.

Colleen headed toward the red awning of Mano's. Gillian was sitting at a table near the window. She stood as Colleen walked in, took Colleen's hand, and kissed her full on the lips.

"You look wonderful," Gillian said. "I've missed you."

Colleen sat down. "You look pretty great yourself. Sorry I'm late, but I had a business call that tied me up for a bit."

"I wasn't concerned. So, how was your day?" she asked as she handed Colleen a menu.

"Mmmm. Food looks good. I think I'll have the salmon."

Gillian laughed. "You're the only woman I've gone out with who has made up her mind that fast."

Colleen put her menu down and propped her chin on her hands. "When salmon's on the menu, I don't need to read anymore."

Gillian motioned the waiter over and ordered for both of them. She chose lobster, but declined the waiter's offer to pick out her own. He soon brought their drinks and a basket of fresh-baked bread.

"My ex-lover got me hooked on this," Colleen said as she squeezed lime into her 7UP. "Didn't know something so simple could taste so good."

Gillian sipped her Chardonnay. "Did you ever drink alcohol?"

"Yeah, in college. Who didn't? But I decided it really wasn't something I liked, so I had my last glass of champagne one New Year's Eve five years ago and that was that."

"I admire that. A woman who knows what she likes."

Colleen looked at Gillian from under her lashes. "Yes, I certainly know what I like," she said, "and so do you."

Was it her imagination, or was Gillian blushing? She almost blushed herself at her own boldness. She reached across the table and ran her nails lightly and suggestively across Gillian's hand.

Gillian cleared her throat. "So, you never answered my question about what you did today."

Colleen smiled and pulled her hand away. "More inquiries about Candy's death. I had a colleague at work check into some people's backgrounds. Did you know that Lori Kestler and her boyfriend are filing for bankruptcy?"

"I did wonder how they were living so well. I've been to Albert's gym in Ocean City. Kind of a seedy place and always in such a mess. Weights and towels strewn all over. Machines in disrepair. Mildew in the steamrooms. It would drive Stephan crazy."

"Why did you go there?"

"I was doing an article for some vacation magazine. They wanted me to check out the workout facilities at various resorts along Maryland's Eastern Shore. Needless to say, I didn't recommend The Iron Workout."

"Did you recommend Candy's place?"

Gillian smiled ruefully. "Yes, I did. I came looking for a story and found a love affair."

Colleen toyed with her straw. "Was it a love affair?"

"I thought it was. Well, maybe I hoped it was. It was too soon after Lori. Candy really loved her, you know."

Colleen thought about what Lisa had told her about Gillian. How could she find out without actually bringing it up? She nervously buttered a slice of thick bread and took a bite. The waiter brought their salads. Colleen picked up a forkful and was flustered when blue cheese dressing dribbled down her shirt. She looked at Gillian to see if she'd noticed. By the smile on her face, Colleen saw she had.

"My brother, William, always told me I was a klutz," she said as she wiped the spot with her napkin. "So Gillian, I told you all about me last night. What about you. I know your father died recently. Any other family?"

"My mother died when I was ten. I was an only child and a disappointment to my father. He wanted me to follow in his footsteps, but I chose a career in writing and then became an aerobics competitor." She laughed harshly. "He probably told his business associates that he had no children."

"Did he know about your being gay?"

"Oh yes, I made it a point to tell him. Just another disappointment."

"It sounds like you two didn't get along. Were you estranged?"

Gillian gulped down her wine and motioned to the waiter to bring another. Colleen could tell she was nervous because she only picked at her salad.

"If you don't want to talk about this . . ."

Gillian shook her head. "No, it's okay. Look, I did something very foolish when I was younger."

Colleen waited. They finished their salads in silence. The waiter brought the wine and their meals, and Colleen ordered another drink.

"I was eighteen. Feeling rebellious. Angry. I stole ten thousand dollars from my dad's bank account and went on a wild spending spree. Took a vacation to Mexico and spent my days getting stoned." She

161

stopped and shook her head. "When I got back in the country, he had me arrested at the airport. Can you believe it?"

"You got probation?"

"Yes. Dad thought it would humble me to have to report to a probation officer every month. I couldn't leave the state. I went to NYU and majored in English just to annoy him. Had my first love affair with a woman who played rugby. She got me into sports."

"Why aerobics, though?"

"Well, Julie needed to keep in shape to play rugby." She looked up from her lobster and smiled. "And you have to admit, aerobics certainly keeps a person in shape. Good for the heart. Gives you lean muscles." Colleen nodded her agreement as Gillian continued. "When my probation was over, I hooked into the competitor's circuit so I could travel around."

"I think it's a great story," Colleen said. "When I think of my staid Irish Catholic upbringing —"

"No, don't ever think of it as staid. I envy you your family life. Having siblings is something I've always wanted. My mother was a good woman, and I've missed her. I'd like to say that I miss my dad, but I don't. I was covering a bodybuilding competition in Germany when he died and didn't even come home for the funeral. I was shocked that he left his money to me. Guess the blood tie was too strong. All I have left is a cousin here and there, and we don't keep in touch."

Colleen sighed inwardly. Gillian had unknowingly answered the one question she was most afraid to ask. She wasn't even in the country when her father died. So much for Lisa's innuendoes. "Guess we don't realize how much we take for granted. I think you'd like my parents, Gillian."

"Do they know you're gay?"

Colleen looked down at her plate. "No. I can't bring myself to tell them. I think my sister suspects, but we've never talked about it." She looked into Gillian's eyes. "I'm a coward. Afraid they won't love me anymore."

Gillian patted her hand. "You're not alone, and you're not a coward. Maybe one day, you'll find the courage. Listen, why are we talking so seriously? I wanted this to be a romantic dinner. Do you want to order dessert?"

"How about we go for a walk along the beach and then get some ice cream?"

"Sounds great to me." Gillian called the waiter over and paid the check.

The night was balmy. They walked the crowded boardwalk, and Colleen nudged Gillian as they passed two men who were obviously a couple. They saw several more people who they knew were gay. Some wore Freedom rings. None, however, walked hand in hand, which made her sad.

As if reading her thoughts, Gillian said, "I'd love to hold your hand, but you know it's too risky. At least, up here it is. Maybe once we get down to the gay beach we can try it."

"The gay bashings... Have they prompted the police to provide more protection at the gay beach?"

"In the first few days after each incident, yes, but then they stop the extra effort. You know, you can't really be too harsh on the police. They're a small force to watch over all these summer visitors."

"But the ones I talked to at the station were horrible."

"They're not all like that. Officer Perry has done a lot to change their attitudes, but it's a slow process."

"Yes, he mentioned that Lieutenant Tucker is on loan. David's so handsome, he must drive the gay boys crazy."

Gillian laughed. "Yes, but in this case, he helps us more by not being gay."

Colleen changed the subject. "I'm curious about Candy's family."

"Kind of a tragic story. Candy told me that her parents disowned her when she told them she was gay. I guess she came out in college. She had a younger brother. He and her parents were killed by a tornado when she was in her mid-twenties. They hadn't spoken since the estrangement. It haunted her."

"The police report said she had no living relatives."

"That's true. Her grandmother died about two years ago. Candy had tried to keep in touch, but the woman refused to talk to her. Letters came back unopened. It's the classic story of rejection by one's family."

"That's why I'm so afraid to tell mine."

"But you never can tell, Colleen. Look at Bianca — she's got a whole different story. Her family is completely supportive."

They came to an ice cream stand and Gillian got low-fat frozen vanilla yogurt for herself and chocolate ice cream for Colleen. As they continued their walk,

Colleen suggestively licked her ice cream, hoping for a reaction from Gillian.

Gillian's eyes smoldered. "Naughty girl," she said and pointedly refused to look at Colleen until the ice cream was gone.

As they neared the end of the boardwalk, more of the couples were gay. Colleen felt safe enough to take Gillian's hand. Their fingers curled together. Colleen could feel the breeze off the ocean whip up her carefully coifed hair and turn it into its usual disheveled mess.

Colleen noticed two men sitting on a bench. One was extremely thin and frail. She could see the disfiguring dark patches of Kaposi's sarcoma on his face and neck. His partner gently tucked a blanket around his legs. He then leaned back and placed his arm across the back of the bench. His fingers rested lightly on the shoulders of his sick lover. Together they looked peacefully out at the ocean. Colleen could feel her tears well up.

Gillian held tighter to Colleen's hand, as if she sensed Colleen's melancholy. "Stephan and Phillip will be home soon," she said quietly. "I can't wait for you to meet Phillip. He's wonderful, and a talented musician."

Colleen couldn't speak. Her throat felt tight, and she knew she'd cry if she tried to talk. They reached the end of the boardwalk and automatically turned left to go down the stairs to the sand. Together they sat on the last step and took off their shoes. They both rolled up their jeans and headed out toward the water.

In unspoken agreement, they talked no more that

night of troubling things. Instead, they played like children, running in and out of the waves splashing up on shore. They fell laughing into the sand and rolled into each other's arms. Covered with sand, they kissed deeply, and Colleen could taste the salt from the sea spray off the water. Gillian teased her, daring her to go skinny dipping in the ocean. But Colleen was afraid of the water at night and shook her head, even though a couple of other people were far out in the water, trying to catch the waves as they rolled ashore.

It was almost midnight when Gillian led her back to the hotel. Gillian's mouth and fingers worked their magic, and Colleen drifted into a world of swirling colors and light and ecstasy.

CHAPTER 14

Colleen woke early the next morning and gazed down on the face that she had come to love so quickly. She was smart enough to realize that her feelings could be just an infatuation, but she didn't want to believe that. Only time would tell. For now, she would believe in her love.

She got out of bed, taking care not to disturb Gillian. In the bathroom, she washed her face and brushed her teeth, thinking about her progress, or lack thereof, and feeling guilty that she hadn't really concentrated one-hundred percent on her assignment.

She still had a lot of unanswered questions, especially about the check she'd seen at Lori Kestler's. It was time to wrap up her stay in Rehoboth, no matter how reluctantly.

Colleen wrote a short note to Gillian and taped it to the bathroom mirror. She'd see her later that morning in aerobics class, but after that she needed to really hunker down and finish things.

The perfect weather of the past week was changed. Dark thunder clouds obscured the morning sun. A harsh wind blew off the ocean, flattening dune grasses and bending sapling trees. Colleen shivered in her light cotton blouse. The buildings lining the boardwalk seemed to catch the wind and throw it back at her. She walked more quickly as sand flung from the beach stung her skin. The boardwalk was deserted. As she passed Bodies By the Beach, her scalp prickled. She glanced uneasily around her. The wind was howling now, sending leaves and sand and paper scraps scuttling across the wooden walkway. Her reflection startled her, staring out from the plate glass window of the gym. Then something else caught her eye. Writing marred the window. No, there had been writing, but someone had tried to wash it off. She looked closer. Yes, at a certain angle she could see the outline of letters. The sight took her back to her childhood. Halloween vandalism. Wax crayon used on car windows. It was difficult to completely wash away. She'd been handily punished for her part.

The letters on the window were big. She traced them with her finger. *Dyke Bitch!* She stepped back as if struck. Even though the vandalism had been mentioned in the police report, it still shocked her.

Colleen looked around once more and then continued on. A few drops of rain splashed on the boardwalk. The wind picked up speed. Huge, roiling waves collided against the shore and retreated, leaving tentacles of foaming water that seemed to reach for her. She started to run. A flash of lightning across the water lit the sky, followed by rumbling thunder. The clouds opened up, sending a deluge of rain. Within seconds, Colleen was drenched. She raced the last couple of blocks back to Paper Nautilus. The rain continued steadily as she fumbled in her pocket for the key. It wasn't there! Suddenly, the door flew open. Denise grabbed her wrist and pulled her inside.

"You look like a drowned rat," Denise said. "What were you doing out on a day like this?"

Colleen dripped and shivered in the entryway. "Just went for a walk and got stuck in the storm. Look, I need a hot shower. I'll be down in a minute, okay?"

Denise moved out of the way. "I'll keep the coffee hot for you."

After her shower, Colleen put on sweat pants and a long-sleeved shirt and went back downstairs. Denise handed her a mug of steaming coffee. Colleen sniffed the aroma. Vanilla again.

"This has got to be the best cup of coffee I've ever tasted," she said, sipping carefully so she wouldn't burn her tongue.

"I still can't believe you went for a walk," Denise said. "It's been crappy all morning. When did you get up? I've been down here for an hour."

"I had to go over my notes on the case. Decided to go out and clear my head. Listen, Denise, can I be honest with you?"

169

"Sure. What about?"

"You've lived here for a while. I know you must have seen or heard things. The gay bashings, the vandalism. Do the police really have no clues?"

"The police haven't been that bad. Sure, there's a couple who are really homophobic, but it seems they're just overworked. David Perry is a great guy. He watches out for us. Unfortunately, he didn't head up the investigation into Candy's death, but I think the cops did the best they could. They check out every incident."

"That's not the impression I've gotten. The guys at the station that I talked to were very uncooperative. The report is sketchy at best. It was almost as if they didn't want to find out what really happened."

"Okay, what do *you* think really happened? Do you believe it's some big conspiracy to hide the truth? If the police dislike gays so much, don't you think they'd welcome the chance to bring more of us down? They grilled Stephan for hours. And Lori too. Come on, your company just doesn't want to pay the money they owe."

"But you implied —"

"I just like to rile things up," Denise interrupted. "Don't pay me any mind. Jenny gets mad at me all the time for causing trouble. I don't know any more about Candy's death than anyone else."

"Sorry. Guess I'm just frustrated. Excuse me, I've got to make a phone call."

Denise put down her mug and grabbed a blueberry muffin. "Don't go blaming the police for a couple of bad apples. I'm gonna go wake up Jenny. See ya."

Colleen watched her bound up the stairs, then picked up the phone. It was early yet, but Lisa should be up. She answered on the first ring.

"Colleen! Where have you been? I tried calling you all last night. That dinner date of yours must have been something else."

Colleen felt the heat rise in her cheeks. "Just tell me what you know."

"I talked to Sampson's secretary." She gave a snort of disgust. "Flirt with him a little, and he's not discreet at all. Told me that Sampson's not above taking a small bribe here and there. Nothing real big — just guiding an investigation along, or not guiding it. You know, like sending certain agents on a case."

Understanding dawned on Colleen. "That's why he sent me on this one. I'm inexperienced. He thought I wouldn't dig anything up."

"Well, I don't believe he thought there was some big criminal cover-up, but if Lori Kestler needs money, she'd want things settled quickly. You said yourself that she isn't physically capable of this particular crime, and you haven't found any evidence showing the death wasn't accidental."

"Did the secretary mention her by name?"

"No, but he did say that Sampson recently bought a new Armani suit and some imported leather shoes. Lori's check could have paid for them."

Colleen thanked her and hung up, then called Brian to check on Smokey. She left a message on his answering machine.

She went back to her room and pulled out her file. She looked at photos of the scene once more. Something nagged at the back of her mind, but she

171

couldn't pin it down. She read through her notes and Lisa's fax. The police report told her nothing new. She wished Stephan were back in town. She just wanted someone to brainstorm with, but she didn't want it to be Gillian again. Colleen decided to go talk to Lori one more time. Maybe she could get her to reveal her association with Kevin Sampson. She'd take her car; the storm showed no signs of letting up.

At the first crash of thunder, Gillian woke and stretched, fully expecting Colleen to be beside her. When she encountered the empty space, she sat up. The suite was silent; no sounds of water running, no radio or television, no kitchen noises. She got up and went to the bathroom. The note taped to the mirror made her smile. There was only an hour until her aerobics class. Then again, it was a perfect day for staying in bed. The thunder rattled her windows. If Colleen hadn't left, Gillian would have called and canceled her class.

She called room service and took a quick shower. Her coffee and cereal with fruit arrived soon after. She got dressed and left for the gym. The rain was relentless, pounding against her umbrella and soaking her feet. Good thing she had a spare pair of Reeboks in her locker. The gym was practically empty. On rainy days, the gym was usually packed, but the morning's driving rain and dangerous lightning had kept most people indoors. The young man who'd opened the gym that morning came out of Stephan's office.

"Hi, Gillian," he greeted. "Just got off the phone with Stephan. He and Phillip will be home tomorrow."

"That's great, Tom," she answered. "Sparse crowd this morning."

"Yeah. Say, Gillian, isn't there an extra set of keys for this place?"

"There should be. Why?"

"You've got your keys, right?" She nodded. "Okay, Stephan took his set with him and he gave me Candy's old set so I could open the gym while he's gone. The alarm key on this set was sticking this morning so I looked for the extra set, but I couldn't find it anywhere."

"I don't remember ever seeing a fourth set, but I know that Candy told me she had one."

"Hmmm. Maybe Candy kept them at her place or something. I'll ask Stephan when he gets back. Ready for class?"

Gillian looked at the three people working out. "These guys don't look like the aerobics type."

Tom clapped his hands to get their attention. "Aerobics start in five minutes," he called out.

The three looked up from their tasks and shook their heads. Gillian shrugged and entered her room. She put a tape in the tape player and sat on the platform waiting for Colleen. It might be interesting to have a private session, she decided. She looked at the open doorway. Too bad it didn't have a door that she could close.

She waited almost twenty minutes, but Colleen never showed up, nor did anyone else. Disappointed, she went into the weight room and decided to work out. Tom was back in the office, working on the

173

computer. Only one other patron remained in the gym. Gillian warmed up with the stationary bike and then the rowing machine. She went to the bench press next. She carefully put forty additional pounds on the barbell and lay down on the bench. She grasped the barbell and lifted it out of the grooves. She broke out in a cold sweat, as she had done ever since Candy's death when she tried to do bench presses. Gently placing the barbell back in the grooves, she sat up and wiped her face with a towel. Her hands were shaking. She could feel her heart beat rapidly against her ribs.

"Are you okay?" the other client asked. He stood beside the bench, concern etched into his face.

She gave him a half-hearted smile. "Yes, thanks. Just took things a little too fast this morning."

"Can I get you some water?"

She stood up. "I'm okay. I think I'll head for the shower."

He looked her over once more before returning to the shoulder press. She watched him a few moments with a critical eye. Satisfied that he was doing the exercise correctly, Gillian entered the locker room. Her heart still raced, her knees trembled. Would she ever be able to do the bench press again without thinking of Candy, and of how she died?

Gillian put the shower on full blast and as hot as she could tolerate it. She stood under the water, letting the needle-sharp spray pound her body. She could feel her heart return to normal. The water pelted her relentlessly, and still she stood motionless. A great trembling seized her. Alone in the cubicle, Gillian allowed the emotion she showed no one to take over. She slid to the floor as great, heaving sobs tore through her. Her hot tears mingled with the hot water that poured down.

Colleen drove through the storm back to Lori's house. The lightning frightened her, moving closer to the land from the open sea. She felt as if she played a walk-on part in some horror flick. The gale force practically ripped the car door from her hands as she got out, the wind slashing her hair against her face. When a gust turned her umbrella inside out, she ran up the sidewalk, past the classic Jaguar, and up the stairs of the Grey Poupon house. She frantically pressed the doorbell as the rain plastered her clothes to her body. The door flew open. Albert Simmons stood before her, a deep frown on his face.

"What do you want?" he growled.

"Please," Colleen shouted above the wind, "can I come in? I just want to talk."

He stood back and let her pass. The door slammed shut and, with the curtains still drawn, the house became dark and eerily quiet. She walked nervously, her clothes dripping a trail of water droplets from the living room to the kitchen. Albert followed close behind. In the kitchen, the window above the sink let in some gloomy daylight. Albert stayed framed in the doorway, but he didn't turn on the overhead light.

She stood shivering on the area rug in front of the sink. "Could I trouble you for a towel and a cup of hot tea?" she asked, teeth chattering.

He disappeared for a few moments and returned with a large towel, which he handed her in silence.

175

She placed her knapsack against the table leg, then dried her hair and wrapped the towel around her shoulders.

"Tea's in the cabinet above the stove," he volunteered, but made no move to get it.

Colleen felt almost as if Albert were guarding her. She filled the tea kettle with water and turned on the gas, playing out a most incongruous domestic scenario. He remained silent as she opened one cabinet and then another, looking for a large mug. She found the right cabinet and took two mugs down.

"Do you want some tea?" she asked, feeling like an actor in some surreal movie scene. He shook his head. "I really came to talk to Lori," she continued. "Is she around?"

"What do you want with her?"

"Just some final questions. I'm ready to wrap up the case, send my report to the office."

"It's about time."

The tea kettle whistled. She poured the steaming water over her tea bag. The aroma of spearmint filled her nostrils. "You didn't answer my question, Mr. Simmons. Is Lori here?"

"No. She's gone for the day. I can answer any questions you might have."

Colleen took the tea bag and dropped it into the sink. She took a sip of the hot liquid. She could feel its heat radiate through her body. She held the warm mug between her hands. She took a deep breath and decided to be frank.

"Okay, Mr. Simmons, I want to know how Lori

knows Kevin Sampson and why she wrote him a check for five thousand dollars."

If he was surprised at her blunt question, he didn't show it. "Simple. We wanted the case settled quickly. The money was a little incentive to Sampson to help us out. Nothing illegal."

"You don't call a bribe illegal?"

"We weren't asking for a cover-up. We have nothing to hide. It was a gift." His bulky frame filled the entire doorway, his huge arms crossed in front of him.

Colleen started to get an uneasy feeling. "Where were you the morning Candy died?" she asked suddenly, without really knowing why.

"I told the police I was here with Lori. She confirmed it. Why are you bringing all this up again?"

Colleen took another sip of tea. She knew she was treading on dangerous ground, but it was as if some unknown force was urging her on. "Were you very jealous of Candy?"

He laughed harshly and uncrossed his arms. He took a step into the room and clenched his fists. "Why should I be jealous of that dyke bitch? If she thought Lori would go back to her, she had another think coming. She certainly couldn't compete with this." His fat fingers cupped his crotch.

His use of the words "dyke bitch" made all of Colleen's instincts scream for her to leave, but she felt frozen. "Did Lori ever talk of going back?" she asked in a hoarse whisper. She cleared her throat.

"Emerson wouldn't stop calling her. Telling her

that I was no good, and that she loved her still. Like some goddamn queer knows what love is. Lori was wavering though, I could tell. I tried to show her the light, that she was going against God's law, but she wouldn't listen anymore."

Colleen wrapped the towel closer around her shoulders. It stirred a memory. Towels strewn about in the police photos of Candy. Gillian's words about Albert's gym. She felt the first rush of real fear — her heart started to pound; her breathing came fast. Albert. Albert was the killer!

In the silence, the rain drummed incessantly against the kitchen window. A flash of lightning illuminated Albert's massive form. His dark eyes had a wild look to them, his lips curled in disgust. The light faded, leaving him once again silhouetted in the doorway. Colleen started to inch slowly toward the kitchen door that led outside. She prayed it wasn't locked.

"I can understand why you might be angry," she soothed as she continued toward the door, "but I'm sure Lori had no intention of leaving you."

"You don't know anything about it. I called that bitch myself, and she laughed at me. Told me I'd never measure up, either as a lover or a body-builder." The loathing in his voice scared her even more. "Just because she won a couple of contests doesn't mean she was better than me."

Colleen was closer to the door. "No, of course not," she choked out.

The door knob was within reach. Heart racing, she reached for it. Albert sprang into the room and was by her side in a flash. He grabbed her wrist. His other hand flashed upward, and she felt a sting against her arm, like the time she'd swum into a Portuguese man-of-war. Letting out a painful groan, she sagged against him, her body paralyzed.

"Where do you think you're going?" he snarled. "Can't have you running out and mouthing off to anyone. Come here."

Dragging her limp and unresisting body over to a drawer, he reached inside. Using Scotch filament tape, he bound her wrists tightly together. Into the living room they went, where she tried feebly to twist away, but his grip was too strong and her body too weak. She fell against a table. The sound of shattering porcelain mingled with the sound of crashing thunder. Albert didn't seem to notice. He yanked her upright as his footsteps crunched into the broken shards.

"I'm not going to mouth off to anyone," she pleaded, barely able to talk. "I have nothing to say. My case is closed."

He didn't answer, but instead dragged her out into the pouring rain to his car. She begged for someone, anyone, to look out their window and see what was happening. He opened the passenger door and shoved her inside, then immediately locked her in. She tried to open it, but her fingers flopped like so many strands of cooked spaghetti. When Albert climbed into the car, she shrank away from him. He only laughed at her as he drove through the storm-ravaged streets of Rehoboth.

CHAPTER 15

Gillian looked at her watch once more and paced her hotel room. It was nearly six o'clock. Colleen had been missing all day, and no one knew where she had gone. Denise had seen her that morning, but Colleen had said nothing about her plans. The storm that swept the coast had kept up its relentless battering for nearly nine hours. Gillian could hear signs of renewed activity on the boardwalk below her open balcony door. She called to the front desk one more time to see if she had any messages. Their answer was the same. Well, she couldn't hang around the hotel anymore. She'd start looking for Colleen in town.

First she went to the Paper Nautilus, hoping Colleen would finally be there. Suzanne and Vera were both in the living room with Shadow. They shook their heads at Gillian's unspoken question.

"I don't understand this," she said. "Colleen wouldn't just leave without telling me."

"She hasn't left," Vera soothed. "Only her car is gone, not her belongings."

Gillian paced the small room. "I need to find David. Do you know if Bianca has seen him?"

"Why get the police involved? What are you thinking?" Suzanne asked.

"Colleen left me a note, saying she'd come to my class. She didn't show, and now I haven't seen or heard from her all day. She takes her car and goes somewhere on the most miserable day of the summer. Don't you think that's odd?"

"Nothing strikes me as odd anymore," Suzanne answered. "We've seen a lot different people stay here, all with their own quirks."

"I have to find David. Can you call Bianca while I go look in Colleen's room? Maybe she left some indication of where she went."

Vera got on the phone as Suzanne took Gillian upstairs. She opened the door to the China Moon and stood in the doorway while Gillian went in and looked around. Gillian couldn't help but smile briefly when she spied the jeans and shirt Colleen had worn the night before. The room was neat, except for the papers strewn across the bed. Gillian walked over and picked one up. She read her name. The report gave all the particulars about her arrest. Shocked and a little angry, she threw the paper down and snatched up another. It was a report on Barry Charles. Her eyes widened as she read. God, she hoped Colleen hadn't gone to see him. She picked up paper after paper. Lori, Stephan, Albert, Robbie. Even Jenny and Denise. Colleen had information on all of them that Gillian hadn't even known it was possible to obtain. What ever happened to good old-fashioned privacy?

Gillian gestured toward the mess on the bed. "Did you know Colleen had all of this stuff?" she asked Suzanne.

"I don't go through my guests' belongings," Suzanne admonished. "She's an investigator. Why are you surprised?"

"I guess I'm not really. It's just that my name's in there too." She paused. "That's to be expected I suppose, given that I was involved with Candy. Do you mind if I stay up here for a bit? I promise to lock the door when I leave."

Suzanne was hesitant. "It's against my rules . . ."

"Just a few minutes. Please?"

Vera's voice carried up the stairway. "Gillian? Suzanne? David is on his way over. Bianca found him at home."

Suzanne looked at Gillian meaningfully, then headed down the hallway to the stairs. Gillian could hear their murmuring voices. She closed the door to Colleen's room and sat on the bed. She ignored the file on Candy's death, going instead for the photos that lay hidden beneath it. She gasped in horror and dropped the photos as if burned. They were photos of

Candy, grim photos that showed her beautiful face defiled by death.

Gillian's hands shook as she picked the photos up again. She went through them one by one, each more disturbing than the next. One photo triggered a memory. She looked carefully at the weights on the barbell. The way the plates were arranged didn't look right. They started symmetrical, then were of haphazard size and not balanced. That would make the weight unevenly distributed. Candy would never have done bench presses in such a fashion. Gillian wrinkled her brow in concentration, remembering how Candy used to work out. She always loaded the plates symmetrically — starting small, then replacing them with the larger ones, followed by the small, until they went in a descending line of weight.

Something was not right here. Why hadn't Stephan pointed this out to the police? He'd worked out with Candy often enough. It could only have been the shock of finding her, she concluded. Gillian looked at a wide-angle photo that showed the entire room. A towel lay on the floor near the weight rack. She looked at a close-up photo; she could clearly see Candy's towel under her body. She scrutinized the first photo again. The room was a mess. Dumbbells and plates and more towels lay strewn about the floor. Something clicked in her mind. What was it?

Suddenly, she leaped up, dropping the collection of photos to the floor. "Oh, my God," she exclaimed out loud.

She raced down the stairs, heart pounding. Suzanne and Vera looked up in surprise. "Where's David?" she gasped. "Colleen's in danger."

Suzanne stood up and took Gillian's arm. "Calm down, girl. You're going to make yourself sick. He'll be here any minute. What's wrong?"

Before Gillian could answer, David Perry walked through the door. She grabbed his arm. "Do you have your car?"

"Yes. What's up?"

She tugged at his arm, urging him outside. "You have to call for backup. We need to get to Lori Kestler's house right away. I think Colleen's there, and she's in trouble."

They got into his car and he picked up the radio to request assistance. He slammed the car into gear and headed there, keeping well within the speed limits. Gillian tried to curb her impatience. To take her mind off the drive, she explained to him about the weights on Candy's barbell, how Candy would never have done her bench presses that way. She could tell that he couldn't grasp what she was trying to say. Finally, they pulled up in front of the house just as another police cruiser arrived. A uniformed officer got out and joined them on the sidewalk.

"What's this all about, David?" he asked, clearly annoyed.

"Don't know yet, Joe," David answered. "Ms. Smith here says she has new information about the Candy Emerson case."

Gillian grabbed David's arm and pointed to a raspberry red Saturn adorned with a pink triangle sticker. "That's got to be Colleen's car. I was right. She's here." She raced up the brick walkway and pounded on the door. She was surprised when Lori answered.

"Gillian! What are you doing here?" Lori's pale eyes widened when she saw the police. "Is something wrong?"

Gillian grabbed her arm and shook her. "Where's Colleen?" she shouted.

David and the other officer came up the stairs and pulled her away. David turned to Lori. "Have you seen Colleen Fitzgerald today?"

"No. I've been out. Just got home."

"Do you mind if we look around?"

She nervously backed away from the door. "Not at all. What's wrong?"

"Albert home?" David asked by way of an answer.

"No."

As he stepped through the door, his feet crunched what he thought was glass. He bent down to look. White shards of porcelain littered the floor. "Accident?" he inquired.

Lori looked a little scared. "I don't know. I found it when I came home and haven't had time to sweep it up yet. I thought at first we'd had a break-in, but nothing else is disturbed."

Gillian had swept past them and gone ahead into the kitchen. She met them at the door. "This is Colleen's knapsack," she told them. Lori, David, and Joe looked at her. Lori's pale complexion turned whiter still.

"I don't know how that got here."

"Where's Albert now?" David asked gruffly.

"I don't know. I just got home, I told you."

"The gym in Ocean City?" Gillian demanded.

Lori looked wild-eyed from one to the other. "It's closed now, as of yesterday. The bank is taking possession. We couldn't hold them off anymore with the promise of the insurance money."

Gillian grabbed David's arm. "That's got to be where he's taken her. Let's go."

"Wait a minute, Gillian. We can't just go charging over. I have no jurisdiction in Maryland." He turned to Joe. "Call the Ocean City police. Ask for Mike Holland — he's a friend of mine. Tell him we'll meet him at the Iron Workout."

After Joe left, Gillian confronted Lori. "Albert killed Candy, didn't he?"

Lori started crying. She didn't even seem surprised at the question. "Yes. I mean, I don't know for sure. I began to suspect. But there was nothing I could do. The investigation was over. I was afraid to confront him. He got so angry whenever Candy's name was even mentioned — I even had to hide *The Whale* anytime an article about her appeared."

"Just because the investigation was officially closed doesn't mean you couldn't have come to the police with new information," David gently reminded her.

"I tried once," she sobbed. "I called and was put on hold. Albert came in and demanded to know what I was doing. I had to hang up because I couldn't think fast enough. He accused me of calling another woman. He threatened to hit me. He said if I left him he'd kill me. I never got up the nerve again."

Gillian wasn't moved by her tears. She was only filled with a rage she hadn't known she possessed. Deep in her heart she knew Lori wasn't really to blame, but now she could only hate her. "Why did you lie for him about where he was that morning?"

"I didn't lie. He told me he was working out in the basement. I had no reason to think otherwise."

"Let's get out of here," Gillian said to David through clenched teeth.

David told Lori to stay in the house and call the police if Albert showed up. Then he and Gillian left.

The drive to Ocean City seemed interminably long. The traffic on Ocean Highway was heavy, and when they got to the city, it slowed to a crawl. David found the gym, but there was no parking lot and all the curbside parking was taken. David double-parked the car and they ran down the small litter-strewn alley leading to the gym.

The outside paint was beginning to peel; the letters on the window were missing the I and the O so it read THE RON WORK UT. The inside of the window was covered with brown paper, and the door was padlocked. Gillian futilely rattled the door. She turned to David.

"What do we do now?"

"Is this the only way in?"

She thought for a moment, trying to remember the layout. Fire code regulations dictated that each facility had to have at least two exits. But where was the second door?

"Let's go around to the back."

David stopped her. "Wait a minute. I think we should hold off until Mike gets here."

"It might be too late by then."

"Listen, if Albert wanted to kill her, he'd have done so by now. If she's still alive, any commotion we cause might send him over the edge."

Gillian started pacing like a caged animal. She just wanted to break the door down and rescue Colleen, but David was right. They had no guarantee that Colleen and Albert were even inside.

"What makes you think that Albert had something to do with Candy's death?" David wanted to know. "He and Lori were each others' alibis."

Gillian stopped pacing. "For crying out loud, David, weren't you listening to me at all in the car? Besides, that's the oldest trick in the book. One lover is the alibi for the other. Don't you watch *Silk Stalkings*?"

He hid a smile. "Sorry, don't have cable."

"Okay. It was when I saw the crime scene photos in Colleen's room. I was looking at them and noticed that the plates on the barbell that strangled Candy weren't symmetrical."

"You've lost me already."

Gillian tried patiently to explain to David once more. "Candy was very meticulous about how she loaded her weights. First she'd start out with the small plates. Then she would take them off, add the larger ones, and put the small plates back on. She did this like a ritual until she'd gotten to her maximum weight. The photos showed the plates not only haphazard, but also unbalanced."

"Unbalanced?"

"Yes, one side had more weight than the other. No one doing bench presses would ever do that."

"But what makes you think it's Albert?"

"The photos also showed free weights and towels strewn around the floor. Neither Candy nor Stephan would do that, and Stephan always cleaned up the place before he closed up each night. But I remembered being at the Iron Workout. I have pictures of Albert's gym for a story I was doing; it's a pigsty. When he works out, he never puts anything away. He also loads his barbells without regard to how the plates are put on."

"Why don't you think Stephan pointed these things out?"

"Maybe he was in shock. We all were, and none of us were privy to confidential police photographs." Gillian started pacing again. "Where's that damn friend of yours?"

Right then, a police car drove up. A tall African-American man got out, dressed in the uniform of an Ocean City police officer. Although his eyes lit up visibly when he saw David Perry, he was all business.

"What do we have here?" he asked.

"Thanks for coming, Mike," David replied. "I'm not really sure, but my friend here, Gillian Smith, thinks someone she knows might have been kidnapped and brought to this gym."

Mike raised his perfectly arched eyebrows. "Have you contacted the authorities?"

Gillian interrupted. "There's no time for formalities. Listen, Colleen's in danger. I know it. We have to get inside."

"I understand your concern," Mike said calmly, "but we can't just go breaking the door down. Do you have any proof that she's in there?"

"C'mon Mike," David said, "can't you cut us some slack here? Let's just go around to the rear exit and see what happens."

"Okay, but you owe me. Let's go."

The three of them trouped around to the back. The area was small and claustrophobic, barely large enough for a garbage truck to back in. A fetid odor exuded from the dumpster, as if it hadn't been emptied for months. The wet and sticky pavement was littered with foul debris. The smell of urine and vomit almost, but not quite, overpowered the smell from the dumpster. Gillian could see the outline of a door on the filth-covered wall.

"God, I wonder when the last fire inspectors came through here," Mike said as he wrinkled his nose in distaste. He had approached the door and was examining it. "Looks like the door has been opened recently."

Gillian pushed past David and immediately tried to open the door. It was locked. She threw down her hands in disgust and kicked at the door. To her surprise, the force snapped the flimsy lock and the door flew open. Without waiting for Mike and David, she ran into the darkness.

The two men followed close on her heels, guns drawn. Their footsteps clattered against cement and then were muffled by short-napped carpeting. They came upon another door and Gillian pulled it open. It was the men's locker room. To the right was the community shower, and to the left the sauna and steamroom. The odor of mildew and unwashed bodies permeated the air. They ran past the rows of lockers and into the gym.

As if on cue, all three stopped at the same moment. Mike motioned for Gillian to stay put, and he and David split up, one going left and the other going right. They pulled their guns as they wound their way among the Nautilus equipment, dodging weight plates and pads and pins. David uttered an unintelligible oath as he tripped on a dumbbell.

Gillian strained her eyes to watch their progress. She hopped from one foot to the other.

Finally, she couldn't stand idle any longer. The least she could do was to find the light switch. Surely the electricity would not be turned off already? She sidled along the wall, palms flat, looking for the switch. The logical position would be near a doorway, but there was none by the door they had come through.

"Hold it right there!" Mike's deep baritone barked out just as Gillian's fingers encountered what she was looking for. She flipped the switch and the gym blazed with light.

CHAPTER 16

Colleen struggled to control her panic as Albert sped out of Rehoboth and headed south on Ocean Highway. The storm still raged all around them. She didn't know what he had hit her with, but her arm still stung and her whole body felt disconnected from her head. Her wrists ached from the tightness of the tape that bound them. She was dizzy, almost disoriented, but cognizant enough to know she was in terrible danger. She tried to stay awake, but consciousness eluded her. Her last vision was of Albert's fierce, determined face as he drove toward some unknown destination.

When next she woke, Colleen found herself lying on her side. Rough carpeting scratched her cheek and smelled as if it hadn't been cleaned in quite a while. She tried to move and discovered that not only were her wrists still bound, but now her ankles were as well. The sharp pain in her arm had dulled to an annoying ache. She rolled onto her back, the intense lights overhead blinding her. Turning her head from side to side, she took in the Nautilus equipment scattered about the room. Despite her situation, she couldn't help but compare it to Stephan's gym, where the equipment was neatly arranged in the order of a standard workout. Everything here looked old and in disrepair — chipped paint, rusted chains, torn padding. The dirty towels draped over several pieces of equipment or lying in heaps on the floor made it look as if the patrons had abandoned the place in mid-workout. An enormous mirror completely covered one wall, brown tape criss-crossing its cracked surface. Directly in front of her, a long counter stretched several feet, its vertical surface plastered with torn posters showing cardiovascular goals and correct weight-lifting procedures.

Colleen inched over to one of the machines. Using it for leverage, she managed to sit up. The place was completely silent. She strained her ears, listening for the slightest noise. Albert must be around some-where. She started biting the tape around her wrists, hoping to rip it loose enough to get off. The poly-nylon fibers resisted her best effort, so she con-centrated on the tape around her ankles instead. She managed to pry one corner loose and began to unwind the tape. Albert must have used the whole roll, she decided, as layer after layer unpeeled.

The sound of a door opening and closing penetrated her consciousness and stilled her hands. The carpeting muffled the thud of footsteps coming her way. A moment of indecisiveness — should she lie back down and pretend to be out cold, or should she remain as she was and confront her kidnapper? Albert's bulk appeared in front of her before she could act.

"So, you're awake," he observed. "I wondered how long you'd be out."

She debated whether to answer him, but decided that was what he wanted so remained silent. He frowned at her, but didn't come any closer.

"You're probably wondering what I'm going to do with you."

She just looked at him, hoping her expression didn't reveal her fear or contempt.

"What, lose your ability to speak? Guess that zapper of mine works better than I thought."

Silence.

He started clenching his fists. "I could just kill you now, but I thought you might want to hear how I killed Candy first. Since you've been so curious and all."

She couldn't control her gasp of outrage. He smiled at his success.

"Thought that might get a reaction out of you." He started pacing. "But you knew all along that I killed Candy, didn't you? You were just playing with me, making me think you're some insurance investigator." He stopped pacing and stared at her, his black eyes blazing with anger and hatred. "You were hired by someone to trap me, weren't you? Thinking you could throw me off 'cause you're female."

She stubbornly remained silent, hoping that he wouldn't lose control and pummel her senseless.

He walked around the gym, absently collecting towels and throwing them into a large plastic garbage can near the counter. "I really tried to make a go of this place," he said conversationally, as if he weren't speaking to a woman whose wrists and ankles were bound with tape. "Had a nice grand opening a couple of years back, the works. All new equipment. But the kind of people that come to Ocean City — they're more interested in the amusement park and the shopping and the beach. Who wants to come on vacation and work out, especially if they're dragging brats along?"

Colleen followed his movements. Pick a towel up, put it in the garbage can, pick another up, into the garbage can. It was almost hypnotic.

"Don't know how Candy made hers such a success. Guess all those queer boys care more about how they look. She was a big draw too. You know, being a celebrity and all."

Colleen felt very strange. Where was this monologue going?

"At first I tried to talk her into a partnership, but she wasn't interested. That was long before Lori, when she first came to Rehoboth. I used to be a pretty good bodybuilder myself, but she was such a snob about the whole thing." His voice took on an angry tone. "Just because I never won any pro competitions, she thought she was better than me, but she wasn't."

He was sweating now. He picked up the last towel, wiped himself off, and threw it in the garbage can.

"The people that came to this gym, they were pigs. Couldn't keep good help either. Irresponsible teenagers! Lori was going to give me part of the insurance money to help me do a complete overhaul. Hire some real professionals. Pay off the bank." He kicked the garbage can viciously. "Bloodsuckers! Can't give a guy a break."

Colleen was beginning to think that Albert had lost his mind. His next statement chilled her.

"I should go to the bank and gun them all down." He gave her a menacing grin. "You know, like that guy in San Francisco who shot all those people."

He walked over to the counter and, with his back to her, began slowly and methodically to rip the posters down. The sound grated on Colleen's nerves. She squirmed uncomfortably; her butt was beginning to get sore. The tape was cutting off the circulation in her hands, but she managed to peel a couple more layers of tape from her ankles before he turned to face her again. He crumpled the shredded paper in his hands.

"Lori came to interview me for a magazine article. You know, another bodybuilder opening a gym in a resort town." He paused for a moment. "Lori compared me to Candy Emerson. That made me angry, but I didn't blame Lori. I thought she was cute. Asked her out. Turned me down flat, then I found out she was Candy's girlfriend." He banged his fist on the counter and made Colleen flinch. "It was my duty to save her from a relationship that could only bring her pain."

Colleen wiggled her fingers, trying to make the blood circulate better. She shifted position, sitting up straighter to take the weight off her tailbone. Albert walked toward her.

"A bit uncomfortable, are you?" he said callously.

He stopped a few feet before her. His menacing size seemed even larger from her angle. He crossed his arms and sneered at her.

"Candy was so easy. I was there all along, and she didn't even know it. Got in using Lori's key. Stupid bitch forgot to ask for it back when Lori dumped her. Turned off the alarm and just waited. Had a bit of a workout first. Wanted to be sure I was pumped up. Know what I mean?"

He flexed his muscles and winked at Colleen. She felt sick to her stomach and finally said, "I don't want to hear this."

He laughed. "Ah ha! So, you can talk. Well, I want you to hear it. I want you to hear every little gory detail so you know how easy you have it when I kill you."

She shuddered. How would she ever escape? Who knew where she was or who she was with? She hadn't told a soul, not even Denise. Maybe someone would see her car at Lori's house. She shook her head. Fat chance.

Albert was talking again. "Yeah, I had a good workout before she came. Felt great. Muscles all pumped up. Kind of turned on too. Always gives me a hard-on." He leered at her. She looked away.

"Candy came in," he continued, "all unsuspecting. I watched her do her warm-ups. I was gonna show her what it was like to be with a real man, but decided she wasn't worth it. Knew it was only a matter of time before she did the bench presses. Even let her do a few sets."

He paused, as if for effect. Colleen kept her eyes averted. She was caught in a nightmare, one that she wouldn't wake up from. She tried to mentally block out his voice, but its sinister resonance penetrated her.

"Got her when she was lifting. She had her eyes closed and I just crept up and zapped her on the arm with my taser. Just like I did you."

Colleen gasped and closed her eyes. The vision of Candy's struggles came unbidden to her mind. She could feel her tears well up, and she squeezed her eyes tight so the tears wouldn't fall. She didn't want Albert to see them.

He seemed to relish the effect his words had on her. She could hear it in his voice. The triumphant bragging. The subtle laughter. The victory. She cried silently, unable to contain the tears after all.

"I pressed the bar down on her throat and she fought like a hellion. Thought she would scratch me. That's when I zapped her again."

Colleen looked up and glared at him. He took a small black object from his pocket and waved it around. "This taser is the best investment I ever made. Shocks a person practically senseless and only leaves tiny marks on the skin."

Tiny marks, Colleen thought. Like insect bites.

"Yeah, this little toy has come in handy a few times. Got a couple of homo boys going at it on the beach once." He laughed heartily. "I wish I'd had a camera to catch the look on their faces. Told them never to come back and left them there with their dicks hanging out."

Colleen wished Albert would just kill her and get it over with. She didn't want to hear any more of his vile stories. He started pacing again.

"So, I added more plates to the barbell to be sure Candy was good and dead. Then I went back home and got into bed. Lori wanted to know where I'd been, but I just told her I was restless and decided to do a workout in the basement. She believed me. Well, why not?" He stopped pacing and looked at her with a lecherous grin. "We had great sex that morning. Took her hard. Got her to fight me."

Great sex? Colleen fought back her nausea. Her mind reeled from all she had heard. Now her feet had fallen asleep. If she survived this, would her hands and feet be permanently damaged?

Unexpectedly, Albert strode over and grabbed her wrists. He jerked her upward, causing her to yelp in pain. She couldn't use her feet to steady herself and fell against the Nautilus machine. He put an arm around her shoulders and half carried her behind the counter, where he dropped her. She landed on her hip bone first, sending a shooting pain coursing through her body. Unable to keep her balance, she fell onto her shoulder and wrenched her neck while trying to keep her head from cracking against the floor. He stood above her, coldly eyeing her as if she were some loathsome insect. She couldn't stand it any longer.

"What are you doing to do?" she croaked.

"Don't worry about it, lady. You're gonna be fish

food." He bent down and rewrapped the tape she had so painstakingly undone. She wanted to cry. "I'll come back and get you tonight. Now, you be quiet."

He cut off a piece of the tape on her ankles and put it over her mouth. She could hardly breathe. As Albert walked away, she almost wished he would stay. Listening to her tormentor would be better than being left alone in a strange place. When he turned out the lights, she wanted to scream, but the tape stuck fast against her lips. She tried to stay calm. As her eyes adjusted to the darkness, the gravity of her situation hit her. She had to do something, but she was so tired. She made a feeble attempt to sit up, but gave that up. Her eyelids closed, and the sleep of exhaustion overwhelmed her.

Colleen had no idea how long she'd slept, but she woke to pitch darkness. She lay very still, listening, wondering how long before Albert returned to finish her off. Who could have guessed that such a simple assignment could turn into something so deadly?

She was able to sit up. The first thing she did was yank the tape off her mouth. It felt like she ripped off half her skin, and she couldn't help the shriek that accompanied her action. The whole lower half of her face felt on fire, but the pain soon subsided into a pin-prickling tingle. She took a few moments to get her bearings. Albert had thrown her behind the counter, which was on the right. The wall behind her and to her left meant she needed to move straight ahead to come from behind the counter. She wriggled forward until she came to the edge, then used it to pull herself up. Using the counter top for support, she rested until she could get her breath and reorient herself.

The dark shapes of the Nautilus machines loomed. She could see the outline of the front door and window; light from the street created a thin border. She could tell that it was dark outside. Night. It was what Albert was waiting for. She didn't have much time. Cursing him to hell, she sat down again and worked at the tape around her ankles. It seemed to take forever, but finally she got it all off. Her arms ached from the effort. As the blood flowed freely, she wiggled her toes to counteract the painful tingling in her feet. Eventually, she pulled herself upright, again using the counter for support.

Colleen knew the locker rooms were down the hall. One of them was bound to have an exit to the outside. She decided to try the front door first, knowing full well it would be locked. Her legs were a bit unsteady, but she strode purposefully across the room and grabbed the door handle. It didn't budge. She bent down to see what kind of lock it had; it would only open with a key. Okay, next course of action.

She couldn't believe her ears when she heard the sounds coming from the direction of the locker rooms. She only needed a few more minutes. Why did Albert have to come back now? Panicked, she looked around for something to use as a weapon. Several dumbbells were scattered around the floor. With her wrists still taped firmly together, she picked up one dumbbell after another, searching for one that she could lift but that would still be heavy enough. She hid behind one of the larger machines. When Albert came in, he would head for the counter. She would be waiting for him.

In the darkness, Colleen stilled her breathing. She watched the doorway intently. A human shape emerged from the hall and paused. She couldn't understand why Albert hadn't turned on the lights, but she was glad for the added advantage. She was so engrossed in watching the form that she didn't see the second one come out, nor the third one that hovered in the doorway before moving slowly along the wall.

She could barely control a gasp as she saw the outline of a gun in Albert's hand. She poised with the dumbbell, waiting for him to go behind the counter. Instead, he headed right toward her. She could feel her panic threaten to overwhelm her. She raised the dumbbell. Stay calm, she admonished herself, as he crept forward, ever closer.

Without warning, the lights blazed on just as a man's voice shouted, "Hold it right there!"

She barely registered the tall black man in police uniform who stood before her, gun raised and pointing at her. Instinctively, she ran straight for him and brought the dumbbell forward and down with all her strength. It connected with soft flesh and hard bone. She heard a muffled curse as he grabbed her wrists to keep her from hitting again. She screamed and twisted to get away, but his grip was too strong.

A familiar voice pierced through her terror. "Colleen! Colleen! It's okay now. We're here."

Gillian? Could that really be Gillian? Colleen opened her eyes and frantically searched the room. The first thing she saw was her own reflection in the wall-sized mirror. Eyes wide with fright, ghostly white complexion, and wildly tangled hair made her look like the banshee of Irish folklore. She turned her head. Gillian and David were moving toward her. She looked up and saw, not Albert, but a man she didn't know. He was dressed like a cop.

"Gillian?" Colleen asked, her voice barely a whisper. Then she fainted.

CHAPTER 17

When next Colleen woke, she found herself staring up at white ceiling tiles and fluorescent lights. She was in a narrow bed and covered with a thin cotton blanket. She could hear the whir and click of numerous machines. To her left, she saw Gillian and David sitting together, heads close as they talked in quiet voices. She could only be in a hospital.

"Hi, guys," Colleen said softly.

Gillian leaped out of her chair and stood beside the bed. She took Colleen's hand. "Thank God you're okay. We were so worried."

Colleen smiled. The warmth of Gillian's hand spread through her own cold fingers. "I am *so* happy to see you." She looked at David, who stood up and joined Gillian next to the bed. "What happened?"

"Well, you had quite an ordeal," David answered. "You can thank Gillian here for figuring out where you were."

Colleen raised her eyebrows in question.

"We have plenty of time to go into that," Gillian said. "The important thing is you're okay. I think the doctor will let you go home soon. He thinks your collapse was the result of stress and exhaustion."

"How long have I been here?"

"Just a couple of hours. It's nearly midnight though," David answered.

Colleen felt a twinge of fear and tightened her grip on Gillian. "Albert?" she whispered.

"Not to worry," David soothed. "The Ocean City police were waiting for him when he returned to the gym. He's in custody. You'll need to give a statement, but that can wait until you feel better."

"Did he confess to killing Candy?"

"Surprisingly, he did. He also admitted to kidnapping you. That's a federal offense, you know."

"What about Lori?"

"The police have her in for questioning, but it looks like she's in the clear. She says she didn't have anything to do with Candy's death, and Albert corroborates that."

"Let's not talk about this now," Gillian admonished. "I just want to get Colleen home and into a hot bath."

"Hey, we forgot to tell her the good news," David said to Gillian.

"Good news?" Colleen asked.

"Yeah. We ran into your buddy Barry Charles in the ER. Seems he was hassling a lesbian couple on the boardwalk — both of whom happened to have black belts in karate."

"Justice is served," Gillian added, and they all laughed.

David patted Colleen's shoulder. "Okay. Let me get the doctor and let him know the patient is awake."

When they were alone, Gillian bent down and kissed Colleen tenderly on the mouth. Colleen felt a rush of emotion that threatened to make her cry. The realization of the danger she'd been in, coupled with her feelings for Gillian, overwhelmed her. She could think of nothing to say and was unable to return Gillian's kiss. Gillian seemed to understand. She sat on the bed and held Colleen's hand.

They sat in silence until the doctor arrived. After a few perfunctory questions, he signed Colleen's release papers and she was on her way back to Rehoboth. She knew she must look a sight and couldn't wait to get out of her grubby clothes and take a hot shower. She wore gauze on her wrists from the removal of the tape. Her whole body felt bruised and battered.

She had so many questions for David and Gillian, but not the strength to ask them. She felt safe cradled in Gillian's arms in the back seat of David's police car. After the raging storm earlier in the day, the night sky was dotted with sparkling pinpoints of light. The crescent moon peeked out from behind wispy clouds. David left the car windows open, and she breathed in the tangy, salty air off the ocean. It was a smell she'd never forget.

David drove directly to Gillian's hotel. Colleen protested half-heartedly as Gillian helped her out of the car and led her through the lobby and up the elevator. David said he would drive to the Paper Nautilus and let Suzanne and Vera know all was well.

Once inside her suite, Gillian sat Colleen on the couch. It didn't seem to matter to her that Colleen's filthy clothes would stain the lavender and pink fabric.

"You sit here while I run you a warm bath," Gillian said as she headed for the kitchen first. "I'm going to make you a nice cup of herbal tea too. It'll soothe your nerves."

Colleen smiled. Gillian was hovering like a mother. Or a lover, Colleen mused. It was a comforting thought.

"Tea would be nice," she answered, "but I think I need something with caffeine."

Gillian peeked her head around the doorway to the kitchen. "You sure? It won't keep you up?"

"I don't think so. Besides, I've slept enough today to last me a week."

Gillian disappeared back into the kitchen. Colleen could hear the sounds of water running, then cabinet doors being opened and closed. Moments later, she brought a steaming mug of tea out and placed it carefully on the coffee table. She also included a plate of low-fat Fig Newtons.

"I'll go fix your bath now," she said.

Colleen patted the couch beside her. "Please, sit for a moment. I just like to have you near me."

Gillian's smile lit up her green eyes. She sat next to Colleen and took her in her arms. Their bodies fit together perfectly. Colleen rested her head on Gillian's shoulder, letting Gillian stroke her hair. As the amicable silence between them lengthened, Gillian took Colleen's chin and raised her face. She leaned down and kissed her, gently at first and then with more urgency. Colleen felt her body responding. She ran her hands over Gillian's breasts and heard her intake of breath. Gillian kissed her cheeks and then her neck. Colleen could sense Gillian's desire and matched it with her own, but then abruptly pushed away. Gillian stared at her in surprise.

"I'm sorry," Colleen said, "but I really need a shower first. I wouldn't feel right making love in my condition."

Gillian laughed and drew her close again. "Your condition? I think you're fine."

Colleen pushed away again. "No, really. I'll be very quick. Promise."

"Okay," Gillian said with a twinkle in her eye. "I'll come get you if you're not out soon enough."

Colleen stood up and held out her hand. "Why don't you come with me?"

The smoldering passion in Gillian's eyes ignited. She stood and urged Colleen into the darkened hallway toward the bathroom. They both stripped quickly and stepped under the warm, pulsing water.

They stood together under the water as Colleen lathered up the sweet-smelling sandalwood soap and let her hands roam over Gillian's muscular body. She loved the feel of those broad shoulders and back, the slim hips, and firm thighs. She slid her fingers boldly into the triangle of dark, curly hair between Gillian's legs. Gillian's answering wriggle and intake of breath pleased her. She reached upward and pulled Gillian's face down for a long kiss. Her fingers curled into Gillian's short brown hair. The water flowed over them, leaving their bodies slick and wet.

Gillian in turn ran her hands over Colleen's softer body. As their kiss deepened, she grabbed Colleen's buttocks and pulled her closer. She knew the wetness between her legs came not only from the water streaming down, but from Colleen's insistent hands and tongue. She moved her hips slowly, placing a knee between Colleen's legs. She thrust forward softly, then with more pressure. Colleen's answering moan increased her desire. She fought the urge to pull her to the floor of the tub and make love to her then and there. She wanted to take Colleen slowly, make her beg for release.

Gillian gently pushed Colleen away and grabbed the shampoo bottle. The scent of almonds wafted into the room as she lathered the liquid up between her hands and then into Colleen's glorious hair. She scrubbed Colleen's scalp carefully, then helped her rinse out. As she prepared a second washing, Colleen took the shampoo bottle from her and returned the favor. The feel of Colleen's nails made Gillian's scalp tickle. She pulled Colleen's hands down and took hold of her unbandaged wrists. Colleen winced and tried to pull away.

"I'm so sorry," she murmured into Colleen's ear before she brought the injured wrists to her mouth for a gentle kiss.

The sight of the nasty bruises brought a momentary anger that Gillian fought to push aside. She would have plenty of time for anger when the time was right, and when she could see Albert face to face. She pushed him out of her mind and concentrated once again on Colleen, letting her hands slide over the soap-slick body to the patch of auburn curls nestled between Colleen's legs.

As Gillian's fingers slid past the hair and thrust into the warm, intimate space she sought, Colleen sagged against her. Gillian smiled. Colleen was wet and ready. She held Colleen with one arm and continued pushing her fingers in and out, slowly at first and then more rapidly. She brought her head down to kiss Colleen's breasts and suck rosy, erect nipples into her mouth. Colleen dug her nails into Gillian's shoulders and then bit her on the neck. A rush of passion surged through Gillian's body. She withdrew her fingers abruptly and dropped to her knees.

Colleen leaned back and used the tile wall for support. Gillian parted Colleen's pubic hair and thrust her tongue in as deeply as she could. She grabbed Colleen's buttocks and pushed her into her mouth, licking and sucking more urgently as Colleen's moans deepened.

Colleen propped one hand against the wall and grabbed Gillian's hair with the other. Knowing that Colleen's position was a bit precarious in their slippery, soapy surroundings, Gillian used all her strength to brace Colleen until she felt the shuddering release she was seeking.

Colleen's moans became more high pitched as her legs twitched against Gillian's chest and her knees

210

buckled. She grabbed Gillian's head with both hands. Gillian could feel the blood pumping through her muscles as she continued to support Colleen. She felt the release of her own orgasm, and then Colleen pushed gently away and collapsed to the floor of the tub. Gillian kissed her eyelids, her cheeks, her mouth, the hollow of her throat. They sat cradled in each others' arms as the water splashed over them like a tropical rainfall.

CHAPTER 18

Colleen pushed through the thick gauze of sleep as she heard her name called. Someone insistently shook her shoulder.

"C'mon, sleepyhead, time to get up. I've got brunch waiting."

Colleen grumbled and turned over, away from the annoying buzz of words. Her tormentor continued to shake her. Finally, she sat up and rubbed the sleep from her eyes. Gillian stood grinning beside the bed. She'd opened the drapes, and the bright sunlight streamed into the room. It was very late in the morning.

"How long have I been sleeping?" Colleen asked with a yawn.

"Well, you missed aerobics, but I suppose I'll forgive you this once."

"Gee, thanks," Colleen said as she threw her legs over the side of the bed. She blushed as she realized she was naked. The dangerous gleam in Gillian's eyes made her pull the sheet up.

"Hmmm," Gillian said, "maybe I should let you stay in bed."

"What, and let your food get cold? But maybe I'll let you entice me into a nap later."

"Deal." Gillian went to the closet and pulled out a pair of jeans and an emerald green polo shirt. "Here, Suzanne got these for you. She felt bad going through your dresser, but I told her you had no clothes here."

"No underwear?"

Gillian gave her a lecherous grin before tossing over a pair of baby-blue silk panties and matching bra. "I love a woman who likes to wear sexy things."

Colleen could feel her face burning. The idea of Gillian knowing the intimate details of her life was still too new. She knew she was crazy to feel that way. After all, they'd shared more intimate things than the color of her underwear. She shooed Gillian out of the room and went to the bathroom to wash up. The sight of the bathtub made her blush again. She caught a glimpse of herself in the mirror and looked more closely.

Did she really look as different as she felt? Her

ice-blue eyes seemed to sparkle with new life, her white skin glowed with a new luminescence. She didn't even mind the freckles that dotted her face. The undisciplined curls of red-gold hair that framed her face suddenly seemed exotic and sexy. She backed away from the mirror and scrutinized her body. For once, her rounded curves were sensual rather than an indication she needed to lose weight. She saw her full breasts in their lacy blue bra the way Gillian must see them.

Smiling, Colleen returned to the bedroom and pulled on the rest of her clothes. She walked barefoot to the living room and was startled to find it full of people. A fancy brunch had been laid out by room service. The long table completely blocked the balcony.

Suzanne and Vera were the first people to reach her. They embraced her in a three-way hug. "We are so glad you're okay," they said in unison and then laughed.

"Believe me, so am I," she replied.

"I can't believe you uncovered the truth about Candy's death," Vera said.

Bianca approached for her hug, "I'm just happy things turned out the way they did."

Colleen noticed a tall, handsome African-American man standing next to David. Then she remembered. He had been in the gym with David and Gillian. But who was he? As if reading her mind, David brought him over.

"Colleen, I'd like you to meet Mike Holland. He's a friend of mine on the Ocean City police department. He helped us rescue you."

Mike took her hand in a firm grip. She

impulsively hugged him. "Glad everything worked out," he said with a smile that reached his dark eyes. "I'll need to take you to Ocean City later to discuss some business, but right now I think this is a celebration of sorts, eh?"

He backed away, and Colleen stepped further into the room. The delicious aroma of the food had made her stomach growl. She realized she hadn't eaten for nearly twenty-four hours and suddenly felt ravenous.

Jenny and Denise each gave her a hug. "Nice goin', girl," Denise said with a light punch to Colleen's arm. "I knew you could do it."

"It must have been so frightening," Jenny said with a shudder. Denise put an arm protectively around her.

Colleen gave a rueful smile. "I'll tell you all the gory details sometime, but not too soon, okay?"

Gillian was waiting for her beside the table. "Here," she said as she handed Colleen a plate, "I took the liberty of giving you a little bit of everything."

"Thanks, love." Colleen took the plate and went to sit down on the couch.

Gillian clapped her hands. "Okay, everyone, help yourselves."

As the others clustered around the table, Gillian sat beside Colleen on the couch. She'd brought over two cups of coffee. Colleen took a few mouthfuls of food and then put the plate down. She wasn't quite so hungry after all. She gestured toward David and Mike standing near the television. "I thought David was straight?"

Gillian followed the direction of Colleen's hand. "Oh, he is, hopelessly so. But that doesn't mean Mike can't wish otherwise. They met when Rehoboth and Ocean City police were cooperating on a rash of particularly nasty attacks on gay men that occurred last summer. Turned out that the same gang of teenagers was responsible in both resorts."

"They'd make a cute couple."

Gillian laughed. "I'm sure Mike has told David that very thing several times."

Just then a knock sounded on the door, and Gillian jumped up.

"Stephan! Phillip! So good to finally see you."

Colleen stood as they walked into the room. Stephan looked a little tired, but otherwise happy. The deep sadness that had always characterized his dark eyes was less pronounced. The painfully thin man that Stephan supported on his arm walked with small, careful steps. He held a cane in his free hand. Colleen knew from conversations with Stephan that he had once been a robust, big man. He still stood tall, with his broad, though now bony, shoulders proudly straight. His sandy blonde hair was cropped short, but Colleen could tell it would be wavy if allowed to grow. His hazel eyes stood out in his pale, angular face and seemed to glow with emotion. Colleen could see the ravages left behind on his body from the insidious disease that was AIDS, but his spirit seemed high. Colleen approached them.

"Phillip," Stephan said, "I'd like you to meet Colleen Fitzgerald. She's the one I told you about. The one investigating Candy's death."

Colleen took Phillip's delicate hand in hers. She could see the fine blue lines of blood vessels beneath the pale skin. "I'm so glad to finally meet you," she said truthfully.

He smiled. "You'll have to let me know what progress you've made."

"You're not gonna believe what's happened," Gillian broke in. She turned to Stephan. "See, you go away for a few days and all hell breaks lose."

"I want to know everything," he said.

"In due time, my dear, in due time," Gillian replied mysteriously.

Phillip sat on the couch and Stephan plumped the pillows behind his back. Their love seemed to infuse the room. Colleen moved away, standing in the entrance to the hallway. She felt the tears in her eyes as she observed them all. Suzanne. Vera. Jenny. Denise. Bianca. David. Mike. Stephan. Phillip. And of course, Gillian. They were her new family. The silent tears fell — happy tears, but sad ones too for Phillip. She hoped she would have time to get to know him.

Gillian looked up from the couch and saw Colleen standing in the hallway entrance. She smiled, her love for Colleen obvious in her handsome face. She raised her eyebrows, questioning. Colleen smiled her reassurance and nodded. Yes, she was okay. Gillian turned her attention back to Phillip. She sat beside him and tenderly took his hand into her own. The others hovered, but he didn't seem to mind.

Yes, Colleen thought, this is my family now.

A few of the publications of
THE NAIAD PRESS, INC.
P.O. Box 10543 • Tallahassee, Florida 32302
Phone (904) 539-5965
Toll-Free Order Number: 1-800-533-1973
Mail orders welcome. Please include 15% postage.

THE BEACH AFFAIR by Barbara Johnson. 224 pp. Sizzling
summer romance/mystery/intrigue.   ISBN 1-56280-090-6 $10.95

GETTING THERE by Robbi Sommers. 192 pp. Nobody does it
like Robbi!   ISBN 1-56280-099-X   10.95

FINAL CUT by Lisa Haddock. 208 pp. 2nd Carmen Ramirez mystery.
ISBN 1-56280-088-4   10.95

FLASHPOINT by Katherine V. Forrest. 256 pp. A Lesbian
blockbuster!   ISBN 1-56280-079-5   10.95

DAUGHTERS OF A CORAL DAWN by Katherine V. Forrest.
Audio Book — read by Jane Merrow.   ISBN 1-56280-110-4   16.95

CLAIRE OF THE MOON by Nicole Conn. Audio Book —Read
by Marianne Hyatt.   ISBN 1-56280-113-9   16.95

FOR LOVE AND FOR LIFE: INTIMATE PORTRAITS OF
LESBIAN COUPLES by Susan Johnson. 224 pp.
ISBN 1-56280-091-4   14.95

DEVOTION by Mindy Kaplan. 192 pp. See the movie — read
the book!   ISBN 1-56280-093-0   10.95

SOMEONE TO WATCH by Jaye Maiman. 272 pp. A Robin Miller
mystery. 4th in a series.   ISBN 1-56280-095-7   10.95

GREENER THAN GRASS by Jennifer Fulton. 208 pp. A young
woman — a stranger in her bed.   ISBN 1-56280-092-2   10.95

TRAVELS WITH DIANA HUNTER by Regine Sands. Erotic
lesbian romp. Audio Book (2 cassettes)   ISBN 1-56280-107-4   16.95

CABIN FEVER by Carol Schmidt. 256 pp. Sizzling suspense
and passion.   ISBN 1-56280-089-1   10.95

THERE WILL BE NO GOODBYES by Laura DeHart Young. 192
pp. Romantic love, strength, and friendship.   ISBN 1-56280-103-1   10.95

FAULTLINE by Sheila Ortiz Taylor. 144 pp. Joyous comic
lesbian novel.   ISBN 1-56280-108-2   9.95

OPEN HOUSE by Pat Welch. 176 pp. P.I. Helen Black's fourth
case.   ISBN 1-56280-102-3   10.95